A HEART IN HEAVEN

Roderick smiled down at her with a tenderness that filled her with joy.

"Dear little girl, you are so young and you think the world is so simple."

"If two people love each other, then the world *is* simple," Louisa protested.

"I wish I could live in your world," he said wistfully. "It sounds such a pleasant place, where only love matters. But the real world is a hard place, my d– "

He drew a sharp breath and checked himself.

"Yes?" she cried wildly, "what were you going to call me?"

"Nothing, I – nothing."

"That is not true." Why can't you say it?"

"You know why. I am a servant. You are a great lady."

"I am *not* a great lady. I am a woman. I want to be loved and I want to give love back. Can't you feel that? Can't you sense it?"

THE BARBARA CARTLAND PINK COLLECTION

Titles in this series

A HEART IN HEAVEN

BARBARA CARTLAND

Barbaracartland.com Ltd

THE BARBARA CARTLAND PINK COLLECTION

Barbara Cartland was the most prolific bestselling author in the history of the world. She was frequently in the Guinness Book of Records for writing more books in a year than any other living author. In fact her most amazing literary feat was when her publishers asked for more Barbara Cartland romances, she doubled her output from 10 books a year to over 20 books a year, when she was 77.

She went on writing continuously at this rate for 20 years and wrote her last book at the age of 97, thus completing 400 books between the ages of 77 and 97.

Her publishers finally could not keep up with this phenomenal output, so at her death she left 160 unpublished manuscripts, something again that no other author has ever achieved.

Now the exciting news is that these 160 original unpublished Barbara Cartland books are ready for publication and they will be published by Barbaracartland.com exclusively on the internet, as the web is the best possible way to reach so many Barbara Cartland readers around the world.

The 160 books will be published monthly and will be numbered in sequence.

The series is called the Pink Collection as a tribute to Barbara Cartland whose favourite colour was pink and it became very much her trademark over the years.

The Barbara Cartland Pink Collection is published only on the internet. Log on to www.barbaracartland.com to find out how you can purchase the books monthly as they are published, and take out a subscription that will ensure that all subsequent editions are delivered to you by mail order to your home.

If you do not have access to a computer you can write for information about the Pink Collection to the following address :

Barbara Cartland.com Ltd.
Camfield Place,
Hatfield,
Hertfordshire AL9 6JE
United Kingdom.

Telephone : +44 (0)1707 642629

Fax : +44 (0)1707 663041

THE LATE DAME BARBARA CARTLAND

Barbara Cartland who sadly died in May 2000 at the age of nearly 99 was the world's most famous romantic novelist who wrote 723 books in her lifetime with worldwide sales of over 1 billion copies and her books were translated into 36 different languages.

As well as romantic novels, she wrote historical biographies, 6 autobiographies, theatrical plays, books of advice on life, love, vitamins and cookery. She also found time to be a political speaker and television and radio personality.

She wrote her first book at the age of 21 and this was called *Jigsaw*. It became an immediate bestseller and sold 100,000 copies in hardback and was translated into 6 different languages. She wrote continuously throughout her life, writing bestsellers for an astonishing 76 years. Her books have always been immensely popular in the United States, where in 1976 her current books were at numbers 1 & 2 in the B. Dalton bestsellers list, a feat never achieved before or since by any author.

Barbara Cartland became a legend in her own lifetime and will be best remembered for her wonderful romantic novels, so loved by her millions of readers throughout the world.

Her books will always be treasured for their moral message, her pure and innocent heroines, her good looking and dashing heroes and above all her belief that the power of love is more important than anything else in everyone's life.

"Love knows no barriers of time, space or age."

Barbara Cartland

CHAPTER ONE
1852

"Quick, quick, come up on deck! We're nearly there!"

Louisa Hatton grasped her friend's hand and did not stop running until they were up in the fresh air, leaning over the ship's rails, gazing at the white cliffs of Dover.

"There!" Louisa cried ecstatically. "There is the coast of England, Arabelle. Soon we will be home."

"I am longing to see your home," said Arabelle Regnac in her pretty accent. She was French, and had become Louisa's closest friend in *L'Ecole des Anges,* the Paris finishing school where they had both spent the last two years. Now Louisa was on her way home, taking Arabelle with her for a visit.

"It's strange to think how I disliked being sent to finishing school," Louisa mused. "I just wanted to stay at home with the dogs and the horses. Oh, Arabelle, just wait until you see our stables filled with so many lovely, lovely thoroughbreds."

"Yes, you have told me about them so many times," Arabelle replied, amused. "My dear friend, you are horse mad."

"Oh, yes," Louisa agreed happily. "I cried at leaving

them. I didn't want to go to 'the School of the Angels'."

"It would be hard to find anyone less like angels than we were on that first day," Arabelle laughed.

"But Mama said I had to learn to be a great lady, ready to take my place in Society. She said if I married a man in a high position, I must be a credit to him and be able to speak French fluently, and preferably Italian and German as well."

At finishing school she had perfected not only languages but deportment and all the social skills. She could play the piano, sing, draw and dance all the fashionable dances.

She also read the newspapers and took an intelligent interest in the world. This of necessity involved a delicate balance.

Her Mama had impressed on her that young ladies were not supposed to appear too clever and must never, on any account, seem knowledgeable about politics. On the other hand, a wife was expected to take a well informed interest in her husband's affairs.

So Louisa had learned to acquire many opinions – and keep them to herself.

Now she was eighteen and ready to face her destiny – whatever it might be.

She had a tall, elegant figure and a pretty face, surrounded by flowing light brown curls. How to dress elegantly was one thing she had gladly learned in Paris. The fashions of the day with their tight waists and huge bustles suited her shape admirably.

Now she was wearing a blue velvet travelling dress, trimmed with braid and a matching blue velvet hat with a cheeky little feather. Her feet were neatly shod in black kid boots and wherever she went heads turned.

It was not just her looks that people admired. She boasted a vivacious spirit and a charm that captivated

2

everyone who met her, and her wide blue eyes held a delightful air of candour and her smile combined innocence and mystery in a way that was intriguing.

More than one young Frenchman had lost his heart to her. Louisa had smiled kindly on them all, but flirted with none of them.

But the other girls at the school had flirted madly. At night they told stories, giggling, about their conquests. Louisa had listened and dreamed.

"And are you going to marry a man in a high position?" Arabelle asked as they leaned on the rail and watched Dover Harbour coming slowly closer.

"I have no idea. It does not matter, as long as I love him and he loves me. What does his position matter?"

"That is admirable," Arabelle agreed, "but a good position is nice too. Perhaps your parents have already chosen a husband for you."

Louisa shook her head, but she could not dismiss this idea as completely as she would have liked. She had always known she was being groomed to make a brilliant marriage. She was her parents' only child and all their hopes were fixed on her.

She was also a little troubled by the visit her Mama had paid her a few days ago to say that she must return home at once.

"But Mama," she had protested, "it's only November. Term does not end until just before Christmas."

"I know, my darling, but I miss you so much. We will go home now."

Her mother's soft speech often lightly concealed a determination that nothing could sway. But Louisa did not think of that at this moment, because Mama's next words were, "and we will arrange a big 'coming out' party for you."

3

Louisa had given a cry of delight and clapped her hands.

"Oh, Mama, I would love it," she said. "But it will be a real grown-up party, won't it? The parties you have given me in the past have been for children."

Her mother laughed.

"You had to grow up first before we could give you a grown-up party," she said. "Now you are eighteen and I promise you will make your debut like a young lady."

"We will give a big ball for you. Then you can take your place in Society and before long we will be planning your wedding."

Louisa had sighed ecstatically.

"Oh, Mama, that will be so wonderful. Will I have a really glamorous wedding?"

"The most glamorous in the County, my darling."

"I want to sweep down the aisle in white satin, with a long train and lots of lace. I will be on Papa's arm and he will be so proud. And there at the altar my bridegroom will be waiting, young and handsome and wildly in love with me, as I am with him."

"I am sure he will be wildly in love," her mother had said indulgently, "but young, handsome men are not so easy to find."

"Oh, no, he must be young and handsome," Louisa had insisted, laughing. "I do so wish I could meet him soon and fall in love in the moonlight and – "

"That is all very well," Lady Hatton said, "but real life is sometimes rather different. Your Papa and I want other attributes in your husband – stability, correct opinions and a high position."

"But Mama, I don't want *you* to find me a husband," Louisa said, astonished. "I might not like him."

"Louisa – "

"Stability and correct opinions? My goodness! Suppose – suppose he is *fat?*"

"He isn't – " Lady Hatton checked herself and finished smoothly, "isn't likely to be fat."

Louisa was too carried away to notice her mother's slip of the tongue.

"Mama, I hope I am a dutiful daughter but I really could not love a man who was enormously fat, however correct his opinions."

"Now, stop this foolish talk. A young girl should trust her parents to know what is best for her."

She looked at Louisa with sudden suspicion.

"I hope that while in Paris you have always been modest in your behaviour, no entanglements, nothing that would make you talked about and damage your reputation."

"No, of course not, Mama," Louisa said meekly.

Her heart had never been touched. She knew nothing about love except what she had read in novels that the girls smuggled into school and read at night by candlelight. The men in those books were all so attractive and real life men seemed dull by comparison.

Now she would be asked to consider marriage with a man whose only virtues were that he was stodgy and boring (for what else could stability and correct opinions mean?)

She gave a little shudder, but only discreetly, in case her mother was shocked.

She had begged to be allowed to bring her best friend, Arabelle, home for a visit.

"After all, Mama, I visited her family. We must invite her back."

Her mother had agreed, although a little reluctantly, Louisa had thought, and when a message had been sent to

5

Arabelle's parents, seeking their permission, it was time to prepare for the journey.

Now the steamer had nearly reached the English coast and Louisa was full of excitement. Because she had spent the summer with Arabelle, it was six months since she had seen her home.

Leaning over the railing, looking at the white cliffs of Dover, Louisa recalled that conversation, and how there had been something strange and troubling about her mother's manner.

"Whatever Mama says, I don't believe she would try to arrange a marriage for me," she asserted firmly.

Arabelle shrugged. Although she was a few months younger than Louisa, she was the more worldly wise of the two. Her favourite occupation was lying on a sofa with a book.

She claimed that Louisa's high spirits and energy left her exhausted. Yet, despite being so different, they were firm friends.

"Would it be so terrible?" she asked. "They would choose a man with money and a title to give you an assured position in the world. Then you could shine in Society."

"But they could not choose a man who loved me," Louisa cried passionately. "Only *I* can do that. I want love – the kind of love which increases year by year.

"I want to feel how lucky I have been to find a husband who loves me like Papa loves Mama. And I want to love him with my whole heart and soul.

"Mama talks about arranging my marriage *sensibly*, but she and Papa enjoy a happy marriage."

"Ah, but were they in love when they married?" Arabelle asked.

"Oh, yes. They say my father was the most handsome young man in the county, with a terrible, wicked reputation."

She said the last words in a thrilled voice. She was too innocent to know much about a wicked reputation, but it sounded exciting.

"Really wicked?" Arabelle asked eagerly.

"Well – he was certainly wild. He gambled and rode dangerous horses and flirted madly with every lady he met."

"That sounds nice and wicked," Arabelle agreed.

"But then he met Miss Sarah Beale and fell so madly in love that he became a reformed character for her sake. She stopped his gambling and once he had married his true love, he never looked at anyone else."

"That is so romantic."

"After all these years they still do little things to please each other. They would not want me to be less happy than they are."

Louisa thought of how secure in each other's affections her parents were. But she also knew that she wanted more than the security of love. She longed also for the excitement of romance.

'But will I ever find what I long for?' she whispered to herself.

There was no chance to muse any more. They had reached the harbour and the clamour and excitement of docking was all around them.

Louisa went below to fetch her mother, who was dozing below deck, attended by her maid.

After a light lunch at Dover they boarded the train that would take them to Surrey and Hatton Place. Lady Hatton, who was not a good traveller, settled herself in the corner of the first class carriage with her smelling salts.

Neither of the girls spoke much for the rest of the journey. They stared out of the window. Arabelle wondered at the beautiful English countryside, covered in the reds, oranges and browns of autumn. And Louisa's heart was full to overflowing with joy at being home again. Soon she would be reunited with her beloved father.

"We're nearly home," she breathed. "Oh, how happy I am! Mama?"

Lady Hatton had been lost in a dream, staring out of the window. Now she gave her daughter a reassuring smile.

"Are you all right, Mama?" Louisa asked anxiously.

"Of course, my darling," Lady Hatton answered quickly.

"I have often thought you seemed sad and thoughtful these last two days."

"It's only the strain of the long journey."

Louisa had a strange feeling that her mother was concealing something, but she did not know what to say.

At last the train was drawing into the little country station. Louisa looked out of the window, curious to know which of the grooms had come to meet them, but there was nobody that she recognised. She saw only a young man.

"It's Blake, our new groom," said Lady Hatton.

"We have a new groom?"

"Three of the others left. Now we have Blake."

"But it takes three men to look after all our horses."

"There's much less work to do," said Lady Hatton hurriedly. "Your Papa has sold some of the horses."

Before Louisa could reply the groom had approached the train. When it stopped he opened the carriage door, bowed respectfully and assisted Lady Hatton down.

"Welcome home, your Ladyship," he said gravely. "I hope you have had a pleasant journey."

"Well enough," Lady Hatton replied. "As you see, I have brought Miss Hatton home and a friend of hers."

The young man bowed to the young girls. Louisa stared in astonishment.

He was the most handsome young man she had ever seen. He was in his twenties, with a lean face, dark brooding eyes and thick black hair. He was almost a head taller than herself, so that she had to look up at him and the impression he made was almost overwhelming.

He bowed again.

"Welcome home, miss."

His voice was beautiful. It held a deep, vibrant, intensely masculine sound. Not the voice of a servant.

Nor did he sound like a servant when he sent porters scurrying to collect Louisa's luggage. He spoke with authority and was obeyed instantly.

Outside the station stood the carriage with the Hatton crest on the panels and two chestnut horses at the front. After letting down the step, Blake offered his hand first to Lady Hatton and then to Arabelle, as the guest.

Now it was Louisa's turn. She placed her hand in the young man's and felt his strong fingers clasp hers. Again she felt the sensation of power and authority, so puzzling in a servant, and looked up.

He was watching her. Two dark eyes gazed straight into hers. Then he looked quickly away, as though remembering that it was not his place to look directly at the daughter of the house.

Louisa climbed thoughtfully into the carriage.

'He looks like the heroes in the books I read,' she mused silently to herself. 'How strange.'

On the way home she asked her mother why so many grooms and horses were missing.

"Your Papa decided that the stable was too large for our needs," Lady Hatton replied. "Of course we still have our carriage horses and a pretty little mare that Arabelle can ride."

"You haven't sold Firefly, have you?" Louisa asked anxiously.

"Of course not, my darling. We know she is your favourite mount. And you ride so well, Papa and I are very proud of you."

"I have heard that Papa was one of the best riders in the County," she said. "I have always wanted to ride as well as he did."

She could not help adding mischievously,

"When you choose a husband for me, Mama, you will make sure he is a splendid rider, won't you? Otherwise I simply won't look at him!"

"Hush, my dear. That was not at all a proper remark to make. What will your friend think?"

"Arabelle thinks as you do," Louisa responded playfully.

"I am very practical person," Arabelle explained. "Romance is delightful, but a title and money matter also."

"I am delighted to find you so sensible," Lady Hatton said. "I am certain my daughter will benefit from your advice."

The carriage horses were covering the ground faster now. The villages flew past. Hatton Spur, Lark Hatton, Hatton End, all testifying to Lord Hatton's importance in the neighbourhood.

At last Hatton Place came into view. Louisa's eyes glowed with love for her home. It was four hundred years old, built from pale grey stone that gave it a beautiful, elegant look. It stood on a slight hill, glowing in the sunset.

'Now I am home,' Louisa thought. 'Could anyone have such a lovely home as mine?'

It was not the grandest house in the neighbourhood nor the most luxurious. But she was sure it was the most comfortable and the happiest.

If she made the great match her parents wanted, perhaps her husband would take her to live in a castle. But no castle could be as beautiful to her as her own home.

"If you had wanted a palace, you should not have married me," Louisa had once heard her father tell her mother.

She would never forget her mother's reply.

"I would have married you, darling, if you had only lived in a cottage!"

'That is how love should be,' Louisa thought.

Her father was watching for them at a window as they drew up. He waved and Louisa waved back.

The carriage halted. Blake came to let down the steps and help them out in the same order as earlier. First Lady Hatton, who was immediately enveloped in her husband's arms. Then Arabelle and after her, Louisa.

As she placed her hand in Blake's and felt his grip, steady as a rock, she had a strange sensation as though warmth and life and masculine vitality were flowing from him to her, through the contact of their palms. It was as though all the vibrant currents of energy in the world were concentrated in the two of them.

For a moment she stood intensely still, held prisoner by a powerful force that filled the whole world. Then the haze cleared and she became herself again, Louisa Hatton, being assisted by a servant. She thanked him graciously and turned to her father.

Lord Hatton was still a handsome man in his fifties, his back straight, his head erect, although there was more grey in his dark hair than she remembered.

11

"Papa!"

"My darling girl."

He enfolded her in his arms and she felt she had truly come home.

She began to introduce Arabelle, but he stopped her.

"Your mother has already introduced me to Mademoiselle Regnac," he said.

Louisa was bewildered. When had that happened? Why had she not noticed?

Then she realised that it must have been while she was holding Blake's hand, oblivious to the rest of the world.

She felt a little frisson of alarm, as though she was no longer entirely herself, but had started to become someone else.

Luckily her parents were too wrapped up in their reunion to notice, but she saw Arabelle regarding her with an interested smile.

As they all walked into the house, she could not but resist looking back to see if Blake was still there. When she saw that he had driven the carriage away, she sensed a strange feeling of disappointment.

Because Arabelle's arrival was unexpected the maids were in a flurry. At Louisa's request she shared her own room with its enormous four poster bed.

"It's almost big enough for four, never mind two," Louisa commented with a giggle. "We can talk all night and have a wonderful time."

"And yet, I wonder if I should have come," Arabelle said. "Your parents are so kind and yet I sense something in the air."

"You mean they don't truly welcome you here?" Louisa asked.

"Oh, no, but there is something – an air of strain – they

have things to say to you that they cannot say when I am here."

"You are imagining things," Louisa maintained resolutely.

Yet a voice in her head whispered that she too had noticed something unusual, something too vague to be defined, but there all the same.

"Come down to the stables with me," she begged, taking Arabelle's hand. "I want to show you my beloved Firefly."

"But we are supposed to be dressing for dinner," Arabelle protested, laughing.

"But Firefly will be hurt if I don't say hallo to her at once." Louisa was pulling her out of the room as she spoke.

But at the head of the stairs they met her mother, who ordered them straight back.

"But Mama – "

"You can see Firefly tomorrow. The maids are already carrying up hot water for your baths. Run along now."

Louisa sighed, as it was so long since she had seen her beloved mare. But she obeyed her mother and soon both she and Arabelle were sitting in tubs having water poured over them.

Afterwards, wrapped in a huge, soft towel, Louisa considered which of her many new gowns to wear. She finally selected one of white silk muslin with a frothy bustle at the back. Around her neck she wore a black velvet ribbon with a single pearl hanging from it.

"Perfect," Arabelle said, regarding her critically.

She too was in white, but with a deep red satin ribbon in the front, which set off her dark hair and eyes. She was not beautiful, but she was endowed with a shrewd little face and a brilliant smile. Her wit was sharp and occasionally disconcerting.

"If he saw you looking like this he would fall in love with you at once," she added.

"He? Who?"

"Who? Anybody. The man you are going to fall madly in love with, who will wipe all others from your thoughts. Perhaps you will meet him tomorrow. Perhaps tonight. Perhaps you have already met. Who knows?"

Suddenly Louisa was back in the moment by the carriage, her small hand held in Blake's muscular one, her senses dazed by the power that streamed from him, while the stars whirled about them. She pulled herself together.

"Arabelle, you really should not talk such nonsense," she chided, trying to sound firm.

"On the boat you were talking the same kind of nonsense yourself."

"Yes, but I didn't mean – "

'*I was not talking about a man who does the work of a groom yet who has the air of a conqueror,*' she thought.

To her dismay she felt a blush overtaking her, not just her face but her whole body, so that every inch of her skin seemed to be alive with a new consciousness, a new aching, urgent need.

She was sure all her shocking thoughts must be obvious to Arabelle's satirical gaze. Yet strangely, when she looked in the mirror, her face was not pink at all. If anything it was rather pale.

"I think we should go downstairs," she said hastily.

Her father came to meet them at the bottom of the stairs, smiling in admiration at the pretty picture they presented and offered them an arm each.

The table boasted a dozen leaves and could seat twenty for huge dinners, but tonight it was at its smallest and seated only the four of them. It was such a beautiful sight, Louisa thought, the pristine white napery, the silver, the lights winking off the crystal glasses and making the warm rosewood shine.

In honour of her first night home she was the guest of honour. Lord Hatton led her to her seat with a flourish before he gallantly showed the other two ladies to their seats.

"Tonight we will be informal," he declared, by which he meant that there were only two footmen in attendance.

The butler poured out the wine and served the first course. Lord Hatton raised his glass.

"To good fortune," he toasted, "to good friends – " nodding at Arabelle, "and to the return of our daughter."

"Oh, it's so wonderful to be home," Louisa said. "I want to know everything that has happened while I have been away."

"We have a new neighbour at Cranford Manor," Mama said.

"Good Heavens!" Louisa exclaimed. "That is news indeed!"

To Arabelle she explained that Cranford Manor was one of the largest and most historic houses in the whole County.

"It belonged to the Earl of Cranford," she said, "but he moved out ten years ago and nobody knows what happened to him. He hasn't been seen for years."

"What about his family?" Arabelle wanted to know.

"He had one grandson," Lord Hatton said. "I never knew him but he was known as the black sheep of the family. He was wild, unruly and always in trouble. He joined the army and nobody has heard of him since."

"You mean he simply vanished?" Louisa asked.

"Completely. He might be in London right now, living a riotous life. Perhaps he is serving abroad. Perhaps he has died. Nobody knows or cares. Cranford Manor has stood empty for years and gradually it fell into a state of disrepair."

"But now somebody has bought it?" Louisa enquired.

"It has been bought by Lord Westbridge," her father explained. "He is apparently very rich and is not only restoring the house, but also making the garden very splendid. People are coming from far and near hoping to catch a glimpse."

"How exciting," Louisa said. "What is Lord Westbridge like? Have you met him Papa?"

She thought her father sounded a little uneasy as he replied,

"Once or twice. He seems an excellent sort of man. He inherited a great deal of money from a relation who lived in the North, but he increases his income by gambling."

Louisa caught a strange expression on her mother's face and wondered if dear Papa had been tempted to gamble with Lord Westbridge. But surely, his gambling days were over?

"He will certainly wake up the County," she said. "Most of our neighbours spend all their money on horses and would rather buy a new horse than a new house."

Her father laughed.

"I dare say you feel the same, my dear. I know you are at your happiest on horseback."

Louisa asked impulsively,

"Papa, why have you sold off so many of our horses?"

"It is time for us ladies to retire," Lady Hatton intervened quickly. "Come with me and leave your Papa to his port."

"But Mama – "

Lady Hatton shepherded Louisa and Arabelle firmly out of the dining room and into the library, where the three of them drank tea for just the right length of time until it was proper for Lord Hatton to join them.

Arabelle was entranced by the Hatton library and climbed the sliding ladder to examine some books on an upper shelf. While she was thus occupied, Lady Hatton lowered her voice to scold her daughter.

"It was most impertinent of you to question your father, Louisa. Gentlemen do not like females who question them and it is essential to do what gentlemen approve. Lord Westbridge would have been shocked if he could have heard you."

"Is it important that Lord Westbridge likes me, Mama?"

"It is important that everyone likes you," replied her mother. "Including Lord Westbridge. He will be coming to dinner soon and I expect you to be at your most charming."

"I promise," Louisa said demurely. "I will ask him to show me his wonderful new garden. I am looking forward to seeing it."

"Splendid. I predict that you and he will get on very well together."

The rest of the evening passed quietly. The ladies were all tired after the journey and were glad of an early night. As soon as the bedroom door had closed behind them, Louisa found Arabelle's mischievous eyes looking at her.

"So he's the one!" her friend said.

"I don't know what you mean," Louisa answered, trying to look indifferent.

"You don't fool me, *Lady Westbridge*!"

"Arabelle, you must not say things like that. Of course he's not – not – "

"Not the reason you are here? To be sure. Why should your parents bring you home weeks early but to meet an

17

enormously rich man?"

"Ssh!" Louisa signaled frantically as the maid entered the room to help them undress.

"My lips are sealed," Arabelle promised solemnly, although her eyes danced. "But I will tell you this, if I had been a beauty your mother would never have let me come home with you."

"I refuse to listen," Louisa exclaimed.

But she could not help remembering the piercing look Mama had given Arabelle before agreeing to invite her.

And in her heart she knew that her friend was right. Her parents had brought her home hoping that she and Lord Westbridge would fall in love and marry and be blissfully happy.

And perhaps they would.

When they had both gone to bed and the light was out, she lay gazing into the darkness, aware that a new and thrilling stage of her life was just beginning.

But when she dozed off, she dreamed of a young man with a lean face, dark brooding eyes and hands strong enough to keep her safe forever.

CHAPTER TWO

Louisa awoke with a start. It was dark and quiet. Arabelle lay sleeping quietly beside her, and beyond their room she guessed that the whole house was asleep.

Slipping out of bed she tiptoed to the window and drew back the curtain a little, revealing a countryside bathed in silver. High above the moon hung in the sky, silent, mysterious. By its light she could make out the stable block.

Suddenly a faint whinny rose into the darkness.

It was Firefly, she thought. She knew the sound the mare made and she was reproaching her mistress for not coming to see her.

'How could I neglect you?' she whispered. 'I am coming, my darling.'

She threw on a cloak over her nightdress, slipped out of the bedroom and down the backstairs to the kitchen. There she found a lantern and lit it. Its weak light would be all she needed.

She crept out of the back door and made a quick dash across the yard to the stables, holding the lantern in one hand and clutching the edges of her cloak together with the other, for the air was cold.

It was very quiet inside and the creak of the door opening sounded very loud. Louisa held her lantern high to look around her and gasped in dismay.

So many friendly faces were gone. Stall after stall that had once been filled with beautiful horses, now stood empty. Even though her parents had told her that they had sold some of the horses, the reality came as a shock.

But her beloved Firefly was still in her stall and whinnied with pleasure at the sight of Louisa.

"It's so good to see you, my Firefly," she sighed. She hung her lamp on a hook, slipped into the stall and rubbed her cheek against the velvet nose. "I am sorry if you felt neglected."

The mare replied in her own way, with a soft whiffling sound, breathing warm air over Louisa and filling her with delight. Full of love, she put her arms around her.

The next moment she was seized by two strong hands that lifted her bodily, hauled her out of the stall and tossed her into a pile of hay like a rag doll.

She fought madly, kicking and flailing, although it was useless while he was holding her off the ground. But when she landed she reacted quickly, leaping to her feet and launching an attack on her assailant.

There was no time to think. She only knew she was in the hands of a vile thug and she must fight to her last breath. So she did, managing to land a punch in his stomach and having the satisfaction of hearing him grunt.

But her advantage was only temporary. This was a big man, powerfully built. He simply lifted her again and tossed her back into the hay. Only this time he dropped down beside her, taking her wrists in his hands and holding her down by the weight of his body, until she gave up fighting and lay there panting.

"Now then," he shouted, "what do you think you're doing here at this hour?"

"*Blake?*"

"What the devil – ?"

His body had been blocking out the light from the lantern. Now he drew back and saw her face for the first time.

"*Miss Hatton?*"

She could have screamed at the picture she must present, her face flushed, her hair tousled like an urchin. Worse than that was the way his body was pinning her down.

Suddenly it was no longer cold in the stable any more. Her body was filled with warmth of a kind she had never known before.

"How dare you!" she exclaimed in a shaking voice. "Release me at once!"

"Yes, miss."

He rose quickly and offered a hand to help her up. Instead of taking it Louisa glared until he dropped his hand and stepped back. While she struggled to her feet, he averted his eyes and fetched her cloak, which had fallen off in the struggle.

She was horribly aware of the thin silk of her nightdress and how she wore nothing beneath it. She wanted to die of shame.

She hurriedly pulled her cloak on, not looking at him, and tried to speak calmly but it was hard when she was still panting from exertion and something else that she could not name.

"I think you must be quite mad to attack me," she cried.

"I didn't know it was you, miss. I thought it was an intruder."

"I had a lamp – "

"Yes, miss, but you hung it outside the stall. It threw the light away from you. All I could see was that someone was in there with Firefly.

21

"You might have been a thief or somebody wanting to harm her. I had to act fast. I didn't hurt you, did I? I am very strong and you are such a slight little thing."

She knew she should reprove him for daring to notice her personal attributes, much less mention them. But she felt battered and bruised all over and there was something in his voice now, a kindness and gentleness, that made her want to lean on him.

"I am just a little scratched by the hay," she replied calmly. "You didn't hurt me."

"I wish I could say the same," he said ruefully. "I've got a big bruise right here," he was rubbing his middle. "You pack quite a punch for a lady!"

In the lantern light she could see his sudden grin and she smiled back. Suddenly it seemed quite natural to be standing in the stable with him, at night, having this strange conversation.

"It is *so* sad to see all the empty stalls," she said, looking around her. "I am used to seeing them all full. Were you here when the other horses were sold?"

"Yes, miss. And you are right, it was sad. They were like friends."

"Oh, yes, they were," she agreed eagerly. "Old and trusted friends. I have known some of them most of my life. I would have liked to have said goodbye."

He nodded. "That's how I felt. I made sure I said goodbye and thank you to each one before they left."

"Did it happen all at once?"

"It took about two weeks. One by one folk came and took them away. Old Frank, who used to be head man, was retired. The other lad was dismissed and there's only me now."

"But why?" she asked, puzzled. "Why did it have to happen?"

"Not my place to ask questions, miss. I am just a hired hand. I sleep up there – " he indicated the ladder into the loft above. "Then I am near in case they need me."

"In case of intruders, you mean?" she asked impishly and they laughed together.

"Thank you for taking care of Firefly," she said.

"I know how much she means to you."

"You do?"

"His Lordship told me. I have been exercising her every day for you. She is a really fine animal."

He walked into the stall, produced an apple from his pocket and gave it to the mare.

"Just a little something to calm her down," he said. "It probably upset her seeing her two favourite people fight."

This was too much.

"Really? You consider yourself one of her favourite people?"

"I know I am. We have got to know each other really well. She trusts me and likes me. After you, of course."

And there was no doubt that Firefly was content with this young man. Watching the mare contentedly munching and then nuzzling him affectionately, Louisa felt her anger with him fade.

"Yes, I can see how much she likes you," she said. "How nice that she has been in such good hands. I am glad I came out to see her."

"You shouldn't have done that," Blake said firmly.

Louisa gasped.

"I beg your pardon!"

"You were very silly to come out here alone at night. If there really had been an intruder or if I had been a ruffian like some stable hands, you would have been helpless. You should take more care."

Louisa's cheeks flamed.

"How dare you speak to me like that!"

"I was just watching out for your safety."

"You are impertinent."

"I am very sorry if I have offended you."

Blake's words were meek, but there was no meekness in his manner. Once again Louisa felt his sense of authority, so strange in a hired hand.

In the half light his eyes were sunk deep in shadow. His mouth was curved and firm and she realised again that this was the most handsome young man she had ever seen. But his impertinence was still inexcusable.

"I appreciate your help," she said with a touch of haughtiness, "but it does not give you the right to speak to me like that. I have a good mind to complain to my father."

"That is up to you, miss."

He was not afraid of her threat and with reason, she recognised. Her father would not approve of her visiting the stables at night and she could not tell him the real reason for her agitation – that this outrageous young man had held her while she was nearly naked and struggled with her intimately, so that she was filled with sensations that threatened to overwhelm her.

The ironic light in his eye told her that he knew he had nothing to fear. Outraged, she felt herself blushing again and it made her even haughtier.

"I and I alone will decide whether I come to the stables or not. There was no intruder and if there had been I could have dealt with him. You said yourself I pack a good punch."

"Yes, and I've felt it. But it didn't stop me oversetting you, did it?"

She gulped with horror. How dare this shameless

creature remind her of how helplessly she had lain beneath him!

"I could have you dismissed," she seethed.

"I don't think so, miss. There are not many men who will do three men's work for one man's pay, as I do. Now I think it's time you returned to the house."

"I shall decide when – "

"I will walk with you – in case of intruders." She sensed rather than saw his grin.

She did not want him to walk with her. In fact, she told herself, she would be happy if he vanished from the face of the earth.

But she was not going to risk another argument with him, so she said coolly,

"Very well, you may carry the lantern."

"Yes, miss," he replied with a suspicious meekness that made her want to throw something at him.

He took down the lantern and went ahead. At the kitchen door he said, "goodnight, miss."

"Goodnight Blake." Remembering her manners she took a deep breath and prepared to thank him for his help. But he simply handed her the lantern and strode away, without waiting to be dismissed.

She ran quietly upstairs to her room. Luckily Arabelle was still asleep. In the darkness she walked to stand at the window. From the stable came a soft, contented, whinny from Firefly and she guessed that Blake must have returned.

She could still feel a faint tingle in her shoulders where his fingers had held her in an iron grip. And not just her shoulders but all over. He had shown no mercy to the 'intruder' and she had been manhandled just about everywhere, as her throbbing flesh reminded her.

No man had ever touched her in such a way in all her

life and it dismayed her to find that, now she was alone, she was not as shocked as she should have been.

She was even more dismayed by the next thought that came into her head.

"If only *he* were Lord Westbridge!"

*

Next morning Louisa was up with the lark, pulling back the curtains to survey the glorious weather. At the sight of the sun bathing the autumnal countryside her mood rose to normal. Last night seemed like a dream.

"You would never know it was November, it's still so mild," she said. "What a day to go riding!"

"Riding!" Arabelle was aghast. "My friend, why must you always be rushing about, *doing* things? It's so exhausting. Yesterday was a long journey. I am going to spend today very gently."

She was as good as her word. Over breakfast she talked about Parisian fashions to Lady Hatton and when she announced that she would rather spend the day at home, her hostess agreed enthusiastically.

Louisa sent a message to the stable to say that she would ride Firefly after breakfast. She had dressed in the new riding habit she had bought in Paris. It was dark blue velvet and showed off the blue of her eyes.

"How elegant you look, my darling," her mother exclaimed. "I am sure if Lord Westbridge should see you, he would fall instantly in love."

It disturbed Louisa to realise that Lord Westbridge was never far from her parents' thoughts. It was as though they had decided already that she was to marry a man she had never met.

Blake appeared at the front door with Firefly. He held another horse and was dressed for riding.

"Blake will go with you," her mother said.

"Oh, no!" Louisa exclaimed involuntarily. She did not want to be alone with Blake until she had recovered her poise.

She managed a merry laugh.

"There is no need, Mama. I have always ridden alone. What danger can there be when everyone here is my friend?"

"But if you were to fall," Lady Hatton protested. "Blake felt – "

"Blake felt?" Louisa echoed, astonished. "Blake is a servant."

"You are not a child any longer," said her Mama. "You must behave like a young lady and take your groom riding with you."

Louisa said no more, but her eyes sparkled with indignation. She was a spirited girl and did not like being ordered about by her groom. He would need to learn that she would not tolerate his presumption.

Kelly, her beloved spaniel, was ready and eager to go with her. He had missed Louisa and had run to greet her when she returned home. Now he was determined not to be left behind.

Kelly too seemed very fond of Blake, she noticed. He gambolled about his feet, demanding attention, until Blake fondled his ears.

"You will be careful not to fall, won't you?" Lady Hatton said anxiously. "If you hurt yourself it will spoil everything."

It was Blake who answered.

"Don't worry, your Ladyship. I will take good care of her."

They rode in silence for a while. Kelly was enjoying himself chasing rabbits. At last they came to a halt on the brow of a hill, from where they could see Cranford Manor in the distance.

"It used to be such a beautiful house," commented Blake.

"And will be again. I understand Lord Westbridge is restoring it to its former glory."

Then Blake made a strange remark,

"He will not succeed. He thinks money can make a house great. But he is wrong."

"Why, what do you know about Lord Westbridge?"

"I – nothing." Blake changed the subject quickly. "Are you angry with me for riding with you, Miss Hatton?"

How beautiful his voice was, she thought. But she must keep him at a proper distance.

"I know you mean only to do your job well," she responded, "but I don't like being molly coddled."

"Many things have changed while you have been away. More than you know."

"Whatever do you mean?"

She thought he was on the verge of saying something, but he drew back, saying quickly,

"It's like Lady Hatton said. You are a young lady and you should behave like one."

"How dare you tell me how I should behave!" she exclaimed, amazed at this freedom.

"If Lord Westbridge saw you riding alone he would not approve. And maybe he would not marry you."

Louisa was amazed.

"And perhaps I would refuse to marry him," she retorted angrily. "Nobody can make me do what I don't want to."

"I do hope you will always think so, Miss Hatton."

Louisa spurred her horse forward. She wanted to get away from this man who knew too much and spoke so freely. When he galloped after her, she increased her speed.

In no time at all they were racing. She felt thrilled by the cold wind whipping past her cheeks.

There was a wall ahead that she had jumped many times before. She leaned low on Firefly's neck, ready for take off. But Blake was catching up with her. At the last moment he reached out and seized her bridle, forcing her to stop.

"How dare you!" she flashed. "My father will dismiss you for this!"

She struggled to make him let go, but Blake grasped her wrist instead, holding her in a grip of steel.

"He won't dismiss me for saving your life," he replied. "The farmer who rents this land keeps a plough behind that wall. It would have killed you."

She grew still. "I don't believe you."

But she did. This man was so strangely sure of himself that she found she instinctively believed anything he said.

He released her wrist. "Let me show you," he said, dismounting and reaching up for her.

She placed her hands on his shoulders, trying not to be too aware of his hands on her waist, ready to lift her down.

"What about your stomach?" she asked lightly. "I believe it was injured last night."

"You do not weigh enough to trouble me," he assured her.

That was another unpardonable freedom, but she could not hold it against him now. Her head swam as he lifted her from the saddle as though she was no more than a feather and set her gently down.

"Come," he said, taking her hand and leading her to

the wall and helping her up onto a large stone that stood at the base, so that she could see over. The plough was indeed there, its sharp teeth gleaming wickedly at her.

Louisa felt faint at the thought of what could have happened to her. She swayed and felt Blake's arm around her waist, keeping her safe.

"I did not mean to upset you," he said gently. "But you had to see it, so that you will know in future."

"If I had landed on that – and poor Firefly – she would have been cut to ribbons. You saved her too!"

"Of course," he said lightly. "I had to think of Firefly."

"Then I thank you for her sake more than for my own. If you hadn't – " She closed her eyes.

"It's over now," he said slowly. "We will go to the village and you can recover."

"I am all right," she murmured. "It's just – "

She drooped against him. How strong he was! How comforting to know that he was there to protect her!

He helped her mount by the simple expedient of fitting his hands about her waist and tossing her lightly up into the saddle. Then they made slow progress to the nearby village of Lark Hatton, where there was Mrs. Birley's Tea Shop.

Mrs. Birley was a kind, elderly lady, who had known Louisa all her life.

She exclaimed over Louisa's pale face, made her sit down and brought her some hot tea and cakes. She even produced some titbits for Kelly.

Louisa looked around for Blake and found him standing by the wall.

"Why won't you sit down over here?" Louisa asked him impulsively. "Are you angry with me?"

"No, Miss Hatton, but I am a servant and you are a lady. It isn't fitting for me to sit with you."

"But you saved my life. Please come in or I will think I have offended you by my rudeness."

Blake reluctantly sat beside her.

"I am not offended," he replied. "But people would disapprove if they saw me like this."

"Then I would tell them that you had saved my life and that you are my friend."

He looked at her admiringly.

"I believe you would," he said.

"I wish you would tell me your name. I cannot go on calling you Blake now we are friends."

"My name is Roderick."

"Tell me all about yourself. What did you do before you came here as a groom?"

"I was in the Army."

Louisa laughed.

"Now I know why you always seem so sure of yourself. You are so good at giving people orders, you must have been a Corporal or a Sergeant."

"Something like that," he said, smiling at her.

"Why did you leave the Army?"

"I was called away by family troubles."

"But you are not with your family now?"

"I – decided I could help my family more by coming here," he said.

"But Roderick, I don't understand – "

"Miss Hatton, you must not call me by my name. If people were to hear, it would harm your reputation."

"Oh, why does a young lady's reputation have to depend on such silly things?" she exclaimed. "Why can't I be friends with whomever I like?"

"Because you are going to be a great lady and marry a

31

man with a lot of money."

"Perhaps. But I would not care about money if I loved him and – and he loved me."

She was suddenly awkward. It was as though the word 'love' had made a blush come all over her. She did not know why. But it seemed to have something to do with Roderick, watching her out of his dark, intense eyes.

"Besides," she added hurriedly, "back there, you spoke of money as though you despised it and the people who possess it."

"I only despise the love of money," he responded gravely. "I have seen the terrible things that it can do to innocent people, how greedy and grasping they can become."

"You don't think I am like that?" she asked anxiously.

He smiled.

"No, you are sweet and kind."

"I wasn't very sweet and kind to you in the stable last night," she admitted.

"I startled you. It was my fault and I am sorry. Are you very bruised this morning?"

"No," she said hurriedly, "no, I am perfectly well, thank you. With his eyes on her she did not want to think about the way he had held her thinly clad body so close to his own strong hard one.

But then she knew she was deceiving herself. She *did* want to think about it.

She wanted not merely to think about it, but to dwell on the thought, reliving it, enjoying it.

It was shameless, immodest, unmaidenly, but she could not help herself.

She tried to look away from Roderick, but her eyes seemed drawn to him of their own accord, and in his eyes she saw a look that she guessed mirrored her own.

He too was remembering, reliving and telling himself that it was forbidden, but unable to stop.

She forced herself to change the subject.

"I wonder why farmer Adams left that plough behind the wall," she mused. "It never used to be there."

"Farmer Adams has gone," Blake said. "When he fell behind with the rent, Lord Westbridge gave him notice and put a new man in at a higher rent."

"What a terrible, hard-hearted thing to do!"

"I warned you that things had changed since you went away. You should take more care. I will not always be there to watch over you."

"Oh, but you must be," Louisa urged eagerly. "When I marry, I shall tell my husband that I want you to continue as my groom. Wouldn't you like that?"

He hesitated. Louisa felt that he was considering thoughts he could not reveal.

"I should like to come with you very much," he replied at last. "But – I don't think I can."

She was about to ask him why. But something in his expression made her look quickly away. Her heart was beating faster.

Mrs. Birley's granddaughter, Jane, came over with a large mug of tea for Blake. Louisa noticed how the girl lingered and smiled at him.

He was such a very handsome man. No doubt there were many girls trying to attract his attention.

'But why should I care?' Louisa asked herself.

Some children came into the Tea Shop. They were laughing and their arms were filled with holly.

One little girl was the daughter of one of Lord Hatton's tenants. She greeted Louisa eagerly.

"Oh, Miss Hatton, it's so nice to see you home again."

"Hallo, Sally. It's very nice to be back, especially with Christmas so near. I see you are getting ready."

"Yes, we've been collecting holly and berries for the Church. And there's going to be a big party in the Church Hall for the poor children. Mr. Blake is helping us arrange it. He has been very kind."

"I'll help you collect more berries soon," Blake promised. "Did you find any mistletoe?"

The child looked sad,

"Yes, but it's on Lord Westbridge's land and he won't let us pick it."

"Shame on him!" exclaimed Blake. He rose from the table. "I will wait for you outside, miss."

He had become a formal servant again and Louisa was disappointed.

'Yet how could it be otherwise?' she asked herself.

The children were eager to talk to her and tell her all the rumours about Cranford Manor and its new occupant.

"He's a wizard," Sally confided in a theatrical whisper, "and he's the richest man in the world, so they say, because all he has to do is wave his magic wand to make money."

"Really? Would 'they' be your grandmother by any chance?" Louisa laughed.

"She says only black magic could explain how he makes enormous amounts of money out of nothing. She says Cranford Manor is a magic palace."

'Evidently,' Louisa thought, 'Lord Westbridge has made a great impression in the district.'

At last it was time for her to go. She called Kelly from under the table and walked out to where Blake was waiting for her with the horses.

As they rode home she repeated what the child had told her.

"Her grandmother is called 'old Sal'," she explained. "She 'sees' things and is rumoured to be a witch!"

"Poor soul!"

"Not at all. She goes out of her way to cultivate the reputation. That way people keep giving her little gifts – cakes, a bottle of wine or two. And every so often she has a 'vision', just to keep everyone interested."

Louisa chuckled with sudden memory.

"A couple of years ago she told me that when I met my future husband, he would be wearing a mask. The following week we had a Christmas party at home with everyone in fancy dress. Some of them wore masks and I went round peering closely into their faces. But they were all too old or unattractive."

"Who knows?" Blake said in a strange voice. "It may happen yet. There is more than one kind of mask."

They rode home by a different route, one that took them across the estate attached to Cranford Manor.

"I remember coming to the house once, when I was a very little girl," Louisa said. "My parents were visiting Lord Cranford, who owned it then. I wandered off into the grounds and got lost.

"I was so frightened and I cried. But then a boy appeared and was kind to me. I think he must have been the gardener's lad. He dried my tears and gave me an apple."

"And you rubbed the apple on your dress," said Blake, "and became upset because it left a mark."

Louisa turned her head to find him smiling at her.

"It was you!" she cried.

They laughed together.

"To think of you remembering me after all this time," he teased.

"I never forget anyone who has been kind to me," Louisa replied simply.

"But you did forget," he reminded her. "You didn't recognise me."

"But you have changed so much in thirteen years."

"Not as much as you have. But I knew you at once. I would have known you anywhere."

They rode on. Louisa felt happy to have found her friend again. All her other friends had been young girls, like herself. But this was a new and exciting kind of friendship.

"Were you there when old Lord Cranford passed away?" she asked.

He was silent for so long that she turned to look at him.

"Yes," he said shortly at last. "I was with him with he died."

"What happened? What misfortune drove him out?"

He was silent again before he said,

"It is a long story, miss. I would rather not talk about it."

"Have I upset you? I didn't mean to."

"I know. It's just that I loved that place and – and Lord Cranford. To see it falling into disrepair and to think of his lonely end is terrible."

"But he was not completely alone," she said impulsively. "He had you and if you were really fond of him you must have been a great comfort."

"Thank you for saying that, miss. I like to think I made it a little easier for him.

"I am sure you did," she said sympathetically, moved by the sadness in his face. "It's all so terrible. A couple of years ago I was out riding by myself and I was tempted to go to the manor and see what it was like.

"I have never seen anything so sad. The grounds were overgrown and choked with weeds. The house itself seemed to be crumbling.

"I managed to scramble in through a window that was falling off its hinges and look around inside. It was ghostly, everything covered in dust and so silent."

"You should not have done that alone," he said. "Suppose you had been hurt and nobody knew where you were."

"I know, it was foolish of me. Mama was very cross when I returned home with dusty clothes and told her where I had been.

"She said I was a tomboy who did not know how to behave like a lady. Soon after that incident I was sent to finishing school."

"And do you know how to behave like a lady now?" he enquired with a smile.

"But of course. I am a perfect lady at all times!"

He did not answer in words, but allowed his raised eyebrows to comment for him. They laughed together.

"I don't know if Lord Westbridge is as fearsome as I have been told," she ventured, "but if he is really restoring Cranford Manor to its former glory, that is one thing to be said in his favour. Don't you think?"

To her surprise, he did not answer and when she turned to look at him she saw that a stony look had settled over his face.

"I could not say, I am sure, miss. Perhaps we should be getting on. It's turning chilly."

Suddenly she stopped.

"Look at that oak over there. It has mistletoe. I want

to pick some for the children."

"It's too high up. Even I could not reach it."

"But I could, standing on your shoulders."

"Miss Hatton, I don't think – "

"Roderick, please obey me," she ordered firmly.

He gave her his knife and crouched down so that she could step onto his shoulder. Then he stood up carefully while she reached for the mistletoe.

"*What are you doing?*"

The cold, grating voice startled Louisa. She slipped, tried to grasp the tree and failed. The next moment she slithered down into Roderick's arms.

They both stared at the tall, dark man with the harsh face, who had appeared from nowhere. He sat there, astride his huge horse and glowered at them.

Above him an oak towered, the branches directly above, so that their shade concealed the upper part of his face.

As if he was wearing a mask –

Roderick set her down and murmured softly.

"This is Lord Westbridge."

CHAPTER THREE

Louisa hastily brushed down her riding skirt and approached Lord Westbridge.

"Please forgive me," she said, smiling. "I should not have picked your mistletoe without permission, but as you are a friend of my father – "

"Who is your father?" he demanded curtly, not allowing her to finish.

"Lord Hatton. I believed we are to have the pleasure of your company at dinner soon."

A change came over Lord Westbridge's face. Temper vanished, replaced by pleasure, but it was a sly, distasteful kind of pleasure that made Louisa uneasy.

He swung himself down from his horse.

"So you are the Hatton filly, eh?" he grunted. "People told me you were pretty." With insolent assurance he took her chin between his fingers and studied her. "They weren't lying."

Disgusted, she only just resisted the temptation to jerk away. This kind of compliment was not at all to her taste, even if he had not breached all the rules of manners by touching her.

There was a cold heaviness about this man that was ominous. He looked as though being unpleasant came naturally to him and that he enjoyed it.

He was in his thirties, tall and lean, with regular features. He might have been attractive but for something disagreeably harsh in his manner.

The thought reminded her of Roderick, who might be in trouble if Lord Westbridge told her father how he had found them. That would not be fair. In order to protect him she addressed him distantly.

"Very well, Blake, you may fetch the horses. I am ready to go home now."

A low growl, almost a snarl, came from Kelly. He had crept up beside her and was staring at Lord Westbridge. A ridge of fur was raised on his back.

"Hush, Kelly," Louisa urged. She was embarrassed at the dog's evident dislike.

"Send your servant away," Lord Westbridge ordered. "I would like to show you my house. Afterwards I will escort you home myself."

"Thank you, sir," she replied politely.

"I will wait for you, miss," Roderick offered stubbornly.

"Be off with you," Lord Westbridge snapped.

The groom did not move. He remained still, looking at Louisa, until she said,

"You may leave, Blake. Please tell my parents where I am going."

"Very good, miss. Kelly."

Roderick mounted, snapped his fingers to summon the dog and galloped away.

For a moment after he had left, Louisa felt very alone and vulnerable. But after all, how could Lord Westbridge hurt her?

As Roderick had done, Lord Westbridge took her by the waist and tossed her up onto Firefly's back, but to Louisa the contrast was stark.

Despite his strength Roderick's touch was gentle. Lord Westbrook threw her up roughly, so that she was made to seize the pommel to avoid falling. This man's touch displeased her as much as his voice.

Nevertheless she forced herself to seem cheerful in his company. On the way back to his house they made polite conversation and Louisa apologised again for picking his mistletoe.

"It is for the Church, you see," she explained.

"My dear Miss Hatton, everything I own is at the Church's disposal – and yours. And I have a very great deal to offer."

She became embarrassed. "Lord Westbridge I assure you – "

"Nonsense, it is what you came to discover. Well, you shall discover everything you want to know."

This blunt manner of speaking was not at all to Louisa's taste. "I think I should be going now – "

But he laid a hand on her bridle, forcing her to stay. "Don't start acting like a milk and water miss, because that annoys me. Look over there. I am restocking the deer herd."

She forced herself to ignore his insolent manner and the sight of deer roaming diverted her. Cranford Manor's deer had once been prized and it was delightful to see them strolling through the misty light, peering shyly through the leaves.

Soon the great house came into sight, a beautiful grey stone building whose origins extended far back into the fifteenth century, although the most recent wing had been added a hundred years ago.

As they neared the house Louisa could see that a great deal of money had already been spent on it. It had suffered badly from neglect, but everywhere repairs had been made.

There was a new roof and new windows and she could see extensive renovation going on inside.

"Everyone is agog to know what you are doing at Cranford," she said. "You are the talk of the County."

"You will be able to tell them all what I am doing," he replied. "Come."

Memories of her secret visit two years ago came back to her as Lord Westbridge led her down a long corridor. It had been empty then, with pale patches on the walls where the pictures had been taken down.

Now there were pictures again, but surely not the same ones as before? These were very valuable. After lessons at her finishing school, Louisa knew enough about art to recognise works by Van Dyke and Holbein and her awe grew.

He led her into room after room, all of magnificent dimensions, all exquisitely furnished, until her head was spinning. When she had seen everything on the ground floor, he led her upstairs, along a corridor and into a room that made her gasp.

It was a very grand bedroom, dominated by a four poster bed, hung with gold curtains. There was more gold in the chandelier that hung from the cream and gold ceiling.

"This is Lady Westbridge's room," he announced.

"You – you mean your wife?"

"Certainly I mean my wife – when she exists. It was designed to be appropriate for her."

"I see, but – " she attempted a teasing tone, "perhaps your wife might find this a little overwhelming and prefer to sleep somewhere less ornate."

Her teasing found no response. He gave her a hard look before saying,

"She will sleep here, in a place appropriate to her status as Lady Westbridge. That is my will."

"But what about *her* will?" Louisa asked.

"We should go down to the library, where I have ordered sherry and cakes."

He strode out, leaving her to follow him. It was clear that he was displeased at having his edicts questioned.

As they walked downstairs he continued to discuss the house in an almost amiable voice, as though the conversation in the bedroom had never happened.

And it had not, Louisa realised with a sudden moment of insight. He had not responded to her final question because he had decided to wipe the whole matter from his mind.

She gave a faint shiver.

"I pride myself that everything is being done properly," he said as they seated themselves in the library. "I never tolerate half measures. I always know what I want. And I always get it!

"This building once dominated the whole district," he continued. "I intend that it shall do so again."

"Do you mean to dominate your neighbours too?" Louisa asked. "Isn't it better to be friends with them?"

"Of course I mean to live on good terms with my neighbours. But any community needs a leader."

"And you see yourself as that leader?" she asked, surprised by his confidence.

"Of course."

She knew it was impolite to argue, but she could not resist saying,

"There are several important families in this area. Suppose they do not accept you as their leader?"

He gave a self assured smile.

"My dear Miss Hatton! You are very young. You know nothing of the world. And that is as it should be.

"But your ignorance, though charming, leads you to make false judgements. I could buy up any family in this district without noticing the cost. They will accept whatever I want them to."

His face was hard with pride and self will.

Louisa remembered what Roderick had said about the love of money and the way it destroyed innocent lives.

It was almost as though Roderick knew something about Lord Westbridge. Something that nobody else knew.

A shiver climbed up her spine. She wished desperately that Roderick could be here now to look after her.

Because suddenly, she was frightened.

When it was time to leave, Lord Westbridge informed her that one of his grooms had already taken Firefly home. They would return together in his carriage.

The carriage was new and very luxurious, with his crest on the panels and the four horses were all jet black, perfectly matching.

"Oh, how beautiful!" Louisa exclaimed and ran to their heads.

He strolled up to join her.

"I have heard you spoken of as a notable horsewoman."

"I love nothing so much as riding."

"I have a mare in my stables that would just suit you. Next time you come we will ride together."

He handed her into the carriage and she was astonished to see that it was piled high with mistletoe.

"I hope you will feel that you now have enough," he said. "If not, I can always provide more."

"That is very good of you," she said.

He smiled. "Do you really think so?"

"But of course. When everyone hears about your kindness – "

He smiled. "Ah, yes, my kindness. Of course."

She recognised that he was telling her that it was not kindness that had prompted him, but some other motive of his own.

He climbed in beside her and the horses started to trot. As they travelled Louisa realised that they were attracting a lot of attention. Carters on the road drew their vehicles to one side to let them pass.

The villagers of Lark Hatton stopped whatever they were doing and stared at the glossy carriage and equipage as it rumbled through the cobbled streets to the little Church.

They halted and Lord Westbridge assisted her down.

"Miss Hatton has brought you something," he proclaimed to the vicar who bustled forward, followed by some of his flock who had been helping to decorate the Church.

"Lord Westbridge has kindly donated mistletoe from his land," Louisa stated, and everyone exclaimed with delight.

Soon the mistletoe was gone from the carriage, but when the vicar invited them inside to see the decorations, Lord Westbridge declined, without consulting Louisa.

"Miss Hatton is tired, we must be going."

He took her hand again to help her into the coach and they drove on. Louisa was aware of the curious looks that followed them. Soon, she knew, the news would be all over the County.

At last they reached Hatton Place. As they neared the house, Louisa saw Roderick watching their arrival, but his face showed no sign of his feelings at the sight of her returning in such state.

How did he feel after the way she had spoken to him in Lord Westbridge's presence? Did he understand that she had only been trying to protect him? She must find him soon and explain.

As Louisa arrived home in glory, her thoughts were all of her groom and how soon she could see him alone to explain her conduct.

Alerted by a footman, her parents hurried out to greet them. Roderick came forward to take the horses' heads. He did not look at Louisa but stood motionless, the perfect servant.

"I have been meeting your delightful daughter," Lord Westbridge declared. "She used her arts to persuade me to give mistletoe to the Church and as her arts are considerable, of course I succumbed."

These words covered Louisa with confusion. What must Roderick think, hearing this man boast of how she had used 'her arts' to entice him?

But her parents seemed overcome with joy, thanking Lord Westbridge repeatedly for bringing Louisa home and inviting him in 'to partake of refreshment'.

He courteously declined and said he would see them the following evening.

"I shall look forward to it," he said, raising Louisa's hand to his lips. "May I hope that you too will look forward with pleasure?"

If only she could snatch her hand away so that he could not kiss it under Roderick's gaze. But politeness forced her to smile and utter conventional words about her gratitude for his generosity to the neighbourhood.

When he had departed her mother bubbled over with delight.

"My darling, what a lucky chance that you happened to meet him."

"Congratulations, my dear," gushed her father, kissing her cheek. "You have made a conquest!"

"Yes, it is very obvious that he likes you," Lady Hatton added.

"But I am not sure that I like him," Louisa objected.

"Nonsense," her mother corrected her quickly. "It is too soon to know how you feel. When you meet him again at our dinner party, you will get to know him better."

"But will I like him better?" Louisa mused.

"Of course you will," Lord Hatton said, quite sharply.

Louisa stared at her father. She was beginning to feel very uneasy indeed.

"Where are you going?" her Mama asked, as Louisa turned back to the front door.

"Just to the stables, Mama. I want to see that Firefly returned home safely."

"She did," her mother said. "I saw Blake lead her in. Go upstairs and change. We need to discuss preparations for tomorrow's dinner and what you will wear."

"Can't I just go to see Firefly?" Louisa urged. She felt she would go mad if she could not talk to Roderick.

"Not now," Lady Hatton asserted firmly.

"But Mama – "

"Louisa, I do not know what has come over you. You never used to argue with your parents."

"Excuse me, my Lady."

Roderick had appeared from the back of the house. "The maid said you wanted me," he enquired.

"Ah, yes. Blake, tell my daughter that Firefly is all right and then you can run an errand for me into the village."

Louisa was in despair. What she had to say to Roderick could not be said in front of her parents.

"I have given Firefly a rub down, miss," Roderick said, giving a slight bow in her direction, but not raising his eyes to look at her.

He spoke woodenly, as though they were strangers. Louisa wanted to cry out. But Mama was watching.

"Thank you," she said politely.

Lady Hatton had scribbled something onto a piece of paper. She gave it to Roderick.

"Go to Mrs. Birley and say I want everything on this list first thing tomorrow morning. Her sweet pastries are the best in the district."

Mrs. Birley's grand daughter, Jane, would be there, Louisa realised. She would smile at Roderick and try to flirt with him. Perhaps he would flirt back.

Louisa clenched her hands. There was an ache in her heart that she could not understand.

Arabelle had been briefly introduced to Lord Westbridge, but apart from that she had stayed in the background, watching everything with a satirical eye. Now she slipped an arm around Louisa's waist and walked upstairs with her.

"He seems to be fabulously rich," she observed when they were in their room. "And you and he make a splendid couple."

"And now the whole countryside has seen us together," Louisa cried in despair. "Oh, Arabelle, I feel as if a net is being slowly tightened around me and there is nothing I can do to stop it."

"Why should you want to stop it? He is handsome, wealthy and puts himself out to please you."

"I don't know – there's something about him – that I cannot like."

48

"Just what 'arts' did you use on him?" Arabelle asked curiously.

"None of course. Now what did you do all day?"

"I have been helping your mother to plan this grand dinner party."

"Oh, it's going to be terrible," Louisa sighed. "They are just parading me in front of him. What will we all sit and talk about?"

"Don't worry, there will be several other people present. All the major families in the neighbourhood are coming, also the Vicar and his family."

"That's a relief," Louisa sighed.

When she had changed her clothes, she sat by the window for a while, hoping to see Roderick return from his errand in the village. But there was no sign of him and at last the two girls went down to find her mother in the hot house where she grew her favourite flowers, even in winter. She was selecting blooms for the table.

Lord Hatton joined them just as his wife had finished giving the gardener her instructions.

"I am determined to set the finest table in the County," she announced. "I am sure that Lord Westbridge is used to only the best. That is why I sent for Mrs. Birley's pastries. I wish our cook could fathom her secret."

Louisa studied the flowers, so that she would not have to look at her mother as she said,

"It is now late. Surely Roderick should have returned by now?"

"Roderick?" her mother echoed.

"I mean Blake. I asked him his first name."

"My dearest, that was most unwise. Blake is nothing but a common working man and you are a lady. You must remember to preserve a proper distance at all time."

Louisa sighed.

"Yes, Mama," she agreed meekly.

"But you are quite right. He is late. I wonder what is keeping him."

"Probably stealing a kiss from Jane," Lord Hatton intervened jovially. "Cosy little armful. Make him a good wife."

"Really, my love," his wife scolded, frowning at this frank speech.

"A young man ought to settle," Lord Hatton resumed. "We have a cottage standing empty. He could marry her before Christmas."

Louisa spoke in a strained voice.

"But perhaps he does not want to marry her. Maybe he doesn't love her."

"Love? My dear girl, that class of person does not have refined sensibilities. I think I will drop him a hint to get on with it."

"I have a headache coming on," Louisa said. "Excuse me."

She ran quickly from the hot house.

It was nonsense. Why should Roderick not marry Jane Birley? The match would be most suitable.

But she wanted to cry.

*

She had no chance to see Roderick for the rest of that day or the next. She began to feel he was avoiding her.

All the servants were busy putting up Christmas decorations, until the whole house looked splendid.

'But why must we lay ourselves out to please Lord Westbridge?' Louisa thought. 'Just because he is rich. That does not mean he will attract me or, even more importantly, excite me.'

She checked herself on that word, suddenly thoughtful. Only a few days ago she would never have thought about whether or not a man could excite her. She knew nothing about such things.

But she knew now.

She had known ever since the night she had struggled with Roderick and felt flames of delight flickering through her body.

This was the secret between men and women and discovering it was like passing through a door and knowing that there was no way back.

But Roderick was a servant. This secret was something a woman should share only with her husband.

Or with the man she loved –

The thought crept into her mind before she could shut it out.

The man she loved.

But that would be her husband, of course.

If her parents had their way, it would be Lord Westbridge.

Louisa covered her face with her hands.

*

On the night of the dinner party Lady Hatton supervised her daughter's preparations, watching as the maid pulled the strings of her whalebone corset.

"Tighter," she commanded.

"Mama, I can't breathe," Louisa protested.

"Just a little further, my darling, to show off your pretty waist."

When the maid had finished, Louisa's waist had lost half an inch and she slipped easily into the new dress her mother had bought her just before they left Paris.

It was made of pink silk with masses of ruffles and flounces, very tight in the waist and low in the bosom. In fact, quite immodestly low.

"Mama," Louisa complained, dismayed by how much of her bosom the dress revealed. "It's indecent."

"Nonsense, my dear," Mama replied calmly. "At night a woman is permitted an amount of *décolletage* that would be scandalous by day. Besides, you need a low neckline to show off the Hatton pearls. Papa took them out of the bank today."

For some reason this increased Louisa's sense of alarm.

"But the family pearls are only worn on very special occasions."

"You will look very pretty in them. They will be yours one day."

"Is this a very special occasion, Mama?" Louisa insisted.

Lady Hatton became awkward.

"I will not hide from you, my darling, that your Papa and I think that Lord Westbridge would make a most suitable husband for you. He is very rich. Ask Arabelle. She has most sensible ideas on this subject."

"You would have everything a girl could want," Arabelle observed placidly from where she was sitting on the window seat.

"Except a husband that I loved," Louisa responded passionately.

"I beg you not to set your face against Lord Westbridge," Mama pleaded, sounding strangely flustered. "You don't know how important – that is, you would learn to love him after the wedding."

"But I want to love my husband before the wedding."

"Not another word now. See what a pretty gift I have bought you."

She gave Louisa a charming fan of spangled pink silk with mother-of-pearl sticks.

"Now, hurry downstairs. Our guests will soon be arriving."

Louisa walked slowly down, her arm through Arabelle's. Inwardly she was very troubled.

Their guests began to arrive. First came Sir Philip and Lady Ainsworth, an elderly couple of great respectability and no offspring. Until now they had always looked up to Lord Hatton as the leader of the neighbourhood. Now that the settled order had been challenged, their nervousness was apparent.

Just behind them came the Honourable James Fanshawe and his lady, followed by the dowager Lady Salton and her brother, an insignificant creature who obeyed his terrifying sister's every word in return for board and lodging.

They were followed by the Reverend Charles Lightly. Although he was a poor man, the Vicar's standing in the neighbourhood guaranteed him a place at the noblest table.

With him was his wife and their youngest son, Simon, a tall thin youth with a serious manner. He had just returned from Oxford University and seemed already weighed down by learning.

Louisa watched their arrival with relief, thankful that Lord Westbridge was not to be the only guest, which would have meant a disagreeable air of particularity.

But Lady Hatton was far too clever for that. She greeted every guest as though he or she alone was the one she was longing to see.

"Thank you so much for letting us bring our boy," the Vicar said to her quietly. "He studies too much and his brain

53

is becoming over-burdened. An evening out will do Simon all the good in the world."

At last they heard Lord Westbridge's carriage arriving. The whole family walked outside to wait for him at the top of the steps.

Roderick was on hand to take the horses. He glanced up and saw Louisa, standing in the light from the doorway.

She sensed a sudden, horrid suspicion of how she must look to him – tricked out in her finery to attract a rich husband. Roderick would think she was greedy for money and status and despise her.

She wanted to sink with shame.

She raised her head. Why should she care what a servant thought of her?

But he was more than a servant. He was a good, honest man. He was a better man than Lord Westbridge. Her instincts told her that this was so.

Lord Westbridge's groom leapt down from the box and opened the carriage door. His Lordship's voice carried to Louisa in the clear air.

"Take the horses to the stable, Benning. This fellow will show you the way."

Louisa hated hearing Roderick called 'this fellow'. Deep in her heart she knew it was not right.

Lord Westbridge ascended the broad steps. He greeted Lord and Lady Hatton politely, but his eyes were fixed on Louisa. She thought she detected a gleam in their depths and it made her flinch.

He took her hand and bent low to touch his lips to her skin. Louisa forced herself to smile.

They all returned to the warmth of the house and Lord Westbridge smiled at Louisa.

"So, my pretty thief, we meet again," he began.

"I am sure my daughter is very sorry for taking your mistletoe," Lady Hatton said quickly.

"I used the term only in jest, madam. Everything at Cranford Manor is Miss Hatton's to command."

Louisa wished he had not made such a statement. It seemed to carry a special significance and her parents thought so as well, because they exchanged glances. Was it her imagination that the guests, too, were casting sly looks at each other?

As the guest of honour, Lord Westbridge should have escorted his hostess in to dinner, but Lady Hatton stepped back, leaving Louisa no choice but to take his Lordship's arm.

The others followed, the Fanshawes, the Lightlys, the Ainsworths and the Saltons, with Simon Lightly bringing up the rear with Arabelle.

At dinner Louisa found that entertaining Lord Westbridge was easy. All he wanted was an audience while he talked about himself and his grand house.

All around the table the local gentry listened with bated breath, as though they already recognised him as their new leader.

"You may ask your daughter, madam, whether Cranford Manor is vastly improved," he said languidly.

Thus appealed to, Louisa replied politely that it was indeed a very fine place.

But she could not resist adding,

"But even when it was shabby, I thought it had great charm."

Lord Westbridge's voice held the hint of a sneer. "You knew it well in its 'down at heel' days?"

"I was there once as a child, when Mama took me to visit the old Earl. Dear Lord Cranford. He was so nice to me. I wonder what became of him."

Lord Westbridge shrugged with cool indifference.

Louisa noticed that her mother was frowning at her in displeasure. She was obviously afraid that Lord Westbridge might be offended.

'I don't care,' Louisa thought rebelliously. 'I do not like him, and I will never marry him. I think I would faint if he ever tried to touch me.'

Lord Westbridge's hands were long and spidery, and the sight of them made her shudder. She thought of Roderick's hands, how shapely and attractive they were, how brown and strong. How reassuring they had felt when they held her.

She knew that Roderick's touch would never make her want to faint.

Then she blushed at her own thoughts. How shocking to be dreaming of a man, wanting him to touch her! Modest girls never indulged in such ideas.

But Roderick could make her think of things that she knew were forbidden.

She became aware that someone had asked her a question, and she had not heard it.

"I – I'm sorry – "

"I was saying that I hoped you would visit my stables and ride an animal that I will provide for you," Lord Westbridge said. "You may recall that we discussed this during your recent visit."

"We didn't exactly – "

"Since then I have given the matter much thought, Miss Hatton. I know that only the finest horseflesh will suffice for you."

"But in Firefly I already have the finest," she parried.

He laughed and again there was the hint of a sneer.

"That animal is all very well. But I will set you on a horse such as no woman ever rode before."

"My daughter is extremely grateful," Lady Hatton intervened, throwing Louisa a scolding look. "She would like very much to try your horse."

Louisa was obliged to smile and nod. But inwardly she told herself that no horse could be dearer to her than Firefly.

If only this wearisome meal would end soon and she could find Roderick.

CHAPTER FOUR

At last it was time for the ladies to leave the gentlemen to their port. Lady Hatton rose and they followed her out of the room.

"Thank you, my dear Arabelle, for looking after Simon Lightly," Lady Hatton said graciously. "I noticed you deep in conversation with him at the table. I fear his talk must be way above the head of a young lady, but you are coping very well."

"Thank you, madam," Arabelle replied meekly.

Mrs. Lightly too wanted to thank her and Arabelle became immersed in talk with the other ladies. Lady Hatton took the opportunity to draw her daughter aside and speak in a low, angry voice.

"Lord Westbridge could not have made his intentions more plain," she said. "Such a flattering conquest and you were almost rude to him."

"But I don't want him as a conquest," Louisa protested. "I did not ask him to come here, sneering at everything I love. I wish he would go away again."

Lady Hatton's face became hard.

"You are a stubborn, stupid girl! How can you judge what is best for you?"

Louisa stared. Her mother had never spoken to her so harshly before.

After that outburst, everything she observed seemed ominous, especially the way Lord Westbridge and her father were laughing as they joined the ladies. They seemed satisfied with each other, as though something had been settled between them.

Lord Westbridge was on his best behaviour, making the rounds of the ladies, being excessively charming, until it was time for the guests to leave.

"You will all be receiving invitations to a ball I am giving at Cranford Manor in the very near future," he announced and there was a murmur of excitement.

At the last moment he lifted Louisa's hand and allowed his lips to linger. She had to repress a shudder.

"I look forward to welcoming you to my home again," he said.

"I shall enjoy visiting you," Louisa said politely but untruthfully.

But she felt that he meant much more than that and she was sure of it when she saw his cold grin.

When the last guest had departed, Lady Hatton bid Arabelle goodnight and drew Louisa into the library. She was very angry.

"I am extremely displeased with you," she said. "All the trouble we have gone to for your sake and you nearly ruined everything."

"But Mama," Louisa pleaded, "I do *not* like him."

Lord Hatton calmed his wife.

"Leave the matter for tonight, my dear. Louisa will think it over and come to her senses."

Louisa ran upstairs and shut herself in her room. She was shaking. She knew now that something was terribly wrong.

"Louisa, what is it?" Arabelle asked. She had just

finished undressing.

"You know what they are planning, don't you? Oh, I cannot bear it." She threw an angry look at her friend. "I suppose you wonder why I care. You think it's all right to marry for money, don't you?"

"No," Arabelle responded softly. "No, I don't think so. And that man is bad. I can sense it just as you do."

"Oh, Arabelle, what *am* I going to do?"

Louisa flung her arms around her friend's neck and they clung together, listening to the sound of her parents mounting the stairs and walking to their room.

At last the house grew quiet.

"Let me help you undress," Arabelle offered. "I have sent the maid away so that we could talk."

"Not yet. There is something I need to do first."

She knew she could bear it no longer. Throwing a cloak over her gorgeous dress, she slipped downstairs and out into the night, running as hard as she could in the direction of the stables.

There was a light on inside as she opened the door. Roderick was there, stroking Firefly's nose. He looked up quickly as she entered and, with her heart beating wildly, she watched his face for a welcome, listening eagerly for his first words.

But all he said, in a bleak voice, was, "you should not be here, Miss Hatton."

The disappointment was so severe that tears stung her eyes. She had longed to see him with such an aching intensity, hoping for so much from this meeting. And he looked at her like a stranger.

"I had to come," she breathed. "I must talk to you. Why have you been avoiding me?"

"I have not."

"Don't deny it. This last few days, whenever I have tried to see you alone, you have just vanished."

"It has been a busy time. I have had errands to run for your parents. I gather a happy announcement is expected at any moment. Should I congratulate you now, miss?"

"How dare you say that to me!" Louisa cried passionately.

"I did not mean to offend you. Everyone seems to think that Lord Westbridge is very suitable."

"Do you think I would ever marry a man I didn't love just because he was suitable?"

"He is immensely rich. Some girls would find that *very* loveable."

She stood before him, challenging him with her fierce eyes.

"Do you think I am that kind of girl?"

He refused to look at her.

"I don't know what kind of girl you are," he said quietly. "I thought I did yesterday. But that was before you put me in my place, in front of *him*."

"But I have been trying to tell you why I did that. When you caught me in your arms I was afraid he would think – "

She stopped because the memory of Roderick's arms about her made her feel suddenly dizzy.

"You were afraid he would think you were over-familiar with the groom and then he might not offer you his hand and his fortune," Roderick said bitterly.

"No. I was afraid he would tell Papa that *you* had been over-familiar and you might be dismissed without a reference. I did it for you, Roderick."

Tears welled into her eyes.

"But you are so horrid, I wish I hadn't bothered," she

added. "I have been trying to explain, but you would not let me. You only have time for Jane Birley."

"Jane Birley?" he echoed, frowning.

"Papa says you are going to make a 'suitable' marriage."

"Am I?"

"Yes, because she's a – a 'cosy little armful', and young men ought to settle down and – and – "

Louisa could bear it no longer. Turning away from him, she burst into violent sobs.

"Don't," Roderick pleaded softly. "Please don't cry."

He gently took hold of her shoulders and turned her round. When she could not stop weeping, he drew her against him so that her head was resting on his broad chest.

"I hope you will be very happy," Louisa sobbed.

"I shall not be happy with Jane, because I am not going to marry her," he replied, sounding amused.

Louisa raised her head. Roderick drew a swift breath at the sight of her tear stained face.

"You are not – going to marry her?" she asked in a trembling voice.

"I don't love Jane. I love – "

She felt a shudder pass through his body, pressed as he was against her.

"Who do you love?" she whispered, hardly daring to breathe as she waited for the answer.

"I love – I love nobody." He repeated firmly, "nobody at all."

She gave a little sigh. "Is that really true?"

"A poor man has no right to love."

"Everyone has the right to love."

Roderick smiled down at her with a tenderness that

filled her with joy.

"Dear little girl, you are so young and you think the world is so simple."

"If two people love each other, then the world *is* simple," Louisa protested.

"I wish I could live in your world," he said wistfully. "It sounds such a pleasant place, where only love matters. But the real world is a hard place, my d– "

He drew a sharp breath and checked himself.

"Yes?" she cried wildly, "what were you going to call me?"

"Nothing, I – nothing."

"That is not true." Why can't you say it?"

"You know why. I am a servant. You are a great lady."

"I am *not* a great lady. I am a woman. I want to be loved and I want to give love back. Can't you feel that? Can't you sense it?"

She knew she had struck home when she felt his hands tighten. With all the force inside him he responded to her, man to woman. He could deny it in words, but not in the tremor in his flesh.

"You can sense it, can't you?" she persisted. *"Tell me the truth."*

"The truth – " he answered hoarsely, "is that you are my employer's daughter, a lady for whom I – have the greatest respect. And that is all."

"It is *not* all," she screamed with all the force of her passion. "You are lying."

"All right, I am lying," he shouted. "There are some things best lied about. Let it be. There can be nothing between us."

"Nothing?" she exclaimed. "Nothing? Look at me Roderick and tell me there is nothing between us."

63

But he turned away as though the sight of her was too much to bear. A mortal man beholding a phantom from another world might have averted his eyes as Roderick did.

"Look at me," she commanded him fiercely. "*Look at me*."

Slowly he turned back towards her, as though unable to stop himself. His face was tortured. As though in a trance, he lowered his head until his lips were almost touching hers. She felt the long, shuddering breath that told of unbearable temptation, a tortured struggle to resist. He was weakening, because she willed it so.

"Roderick," she whispered eagerly, "*Roderick*."

But the words broke the spell. Slowly he released her, looking like a man coming out of a dream. He stood back sharply, as though he was escaping the flames and regarded her luxurious clothes, as if seeing them for the first time.

Louisa nearly cried out as she saw a look of aloofness settle over his face.

"I think you should leave now, Miss Hatton," he said. "And you must never come here again at night. It isn't – it isn't proper."

Her hands flew to her mouth.

"Roderick – " she whispered in anguish.

"Goodnight, Miss Hatton."

Louisa whirled and fled the stable. Tears were pouring down her face as she ran back to the house and upstairs to her room.

There she flung herself down on her bed and sobbed her heart out.

*

The district was abuzz with anticipation. Lord Westbridge had sent out invitations for his great ball at Cranford Manor. Everyone knew it would be the biggest and most glamorous occasion the County had ever seen.

"He is calling it a Christmas Ball," Lord Hatton observed, "but I suspect he really wants to show off his house."

"Papa, must I attend?" Louisa pleaded.

"Don't be absurd, my child," Lord Hatton said. "You are to be the Guest of Honour."

"Oh, no! Oh, please believe me, I don't want that. It looks so – so particular."

"I am losing all patience with you," Lady Hatton said. "The richest man in the County is making you the object of his attentions and you create a silly scene."

"I do not see what his being rich has to do with it," Louisa answered unhappily. "I don't think money matters at all."

"That is because you are ignorant of the world," her mother reproved her severely.

"If I loved a man I could be happy with him in a cottage. Like you."

"Me? When did I ever marry a man in a cottage?" Lady Hatton demanded, aghast. "The very idea!"

"You said once that you would have lived in a cottage with Papa, because you loved him so much."

Lady Hatton breathed hard. She was very angry.

"It is time you stopped indulging in ridiculous dreams," she carped.

"But it was *you* who made me realise that love is more important than money," Louisa said passionately. "Is that a silly dream? Don't you believe it any more?"

Lady Hatton did not answer. She only glared at her daughter and hurried from the room.

"Papa – " Louisa appealed, almost in tears.

"There, there, my dear," he soothed her. "People say these things, but of course nobody wants to be poor. Money is very important. In fact – well, just take it from me that money is vital."

Louisa felt suddenly alone and desolate. She had never heard her parents talk like this before. It was as though they were turning into different people before her very eyes.

She sent a message to the stables that she would ride today and hurried upstairs to dress in her riding habit.

Roderick was waiting for her with Firefly and his own horse, ready saddled so that he could accompany her. But instead of helping Louisa to mount, he pointed to a box in the stable yard.

"Look what I have found," he said. "It's a lady's mounting block. I set it beside your horse, and now you don't need my help."

It was clear to Louisa that he was keeping his distance. He did not even want to help her into the saddle, because it would have meant touching her.

She knew he was protecting her. It was not safe for them to touch, even innocently. But it made her feel sad and lonelier than ever.

As they rode, he kept his own horse well back, instead of riding beside her. At last Louisa slowed to a canter and beckoned him forward.

"Don't keep away from me, Roderick," she said. "You are the only one I can talk to."

"I wish I could help you, Miss Hatton."

"I feel as if a net has been spread out for me, and I am being lured into it bit by bit. I struggle, but it's no use. I don't know my parents any more. All they care about is Lord Westbridge and his money."

"Westbridge is a heavy gambler," Roderick stated,

dropping the 'Lord' and speaking of the man with open contempt. "Perhaps your father owes him money."

"Papa gave up gambling years ago. Besides, my father loves me. He would never – what a horrible idea! Oh, no, it's impossible!"

"Westbridge wants you," Roderick said. "He has done from the first moment he set eyes on you. I know some of his servants and they tell me that he speaks of you as no gentleman should speak about a lady."

"The first day we met, I told you nobody could make me do what I didn't want to do," Louisa reminded him. "And you said you hoped I would always think so. What did you mean?"

"Only that the world is very hard on a girl who has nobody to protect her."

Once Louisa would have insisted that her father would protect her. Now she said,

"But will you not protect me, Roderick?"

He laid his hand briefly over hers.

"In any way I can," he replied seriously. "Trust me. I will always be there for you. Even if you cannot see me."

She raised his hand and brushed her cheek against it. She felt comforted.

But how could that be? Roderick was a servant.

Then suddenly she understood that what mattered was the man inside, not how the world saw him. Some masters had the souls of servants and some servants had the souls of masters.

There was nothing subservient about Roderick. He was a true man, with power and instinctive authority. Her heart had recognised this from the start.

The next moment he proved it by saying quietly,

"I think it would be best if you did not visit the stables

any more at night."

"You don't want to see me?" she asked in dismay.

"Not at night. It's dangerous for you, can't you see that? If anyone were to find out, you would be compromised."

"And then Lord Westbridge would not want to marry me!" she cried with sudden inspiration. "Why that's the answer. Let me be compromised!"

There was a touch of sternness in Roderick's voice as he said,

"You talk like a child. Do you believe that I could bring myself to expose you to danger?"

"But if – "

"I said *no*," he told her firmly.

She stared at him in shocked silence. Then he took her hand and held it fast.

"I think only of you," he said gently. "I have promised to protect you."

He looked at her hand lying in his, before returning it to her.

"And this is the last time I shall ever touch you like this. Now I am going to take you home."

She followed him in silence.

*

Christmas was drawing closer and all the shops were bright with decorations. Holly hung over the doors. The bright scarlet berries made a cheerful show and Louisa's spirits lifted.

It was surely impossible that her worst fears should be realised. It was all a misunderstanding. Nobody could force her to marry Lord Westbridge if she did not want to.

But nothing altered Roderick's grave demeanour. He

kept rigidly to his word, behaving like the perfect groom and no more. Louisa rode every day, just to be with him. Her rides with him made her blissfully happy and wretchedly miserable at the same time.

She dared not mention the feeling that was fast growing between them lest he retreat from her. But sometimes she would glance up quickly enough to catch him looking at her. Then she saw his heart in his eyes and knew that he felt a thousand emotions that he could never speak about.

At other times she would make him take her to the village in the carriage, so that she could do some Christmas shopping. Arabelle would often come with them, but she usually slipped away for an hour. Louisa was glad as it gave her a little time alone with Roderick, although she felt guilty at neglecting her friend.

Arabelle, however, seemed very content to be left to her own devices. Once Louisa glimpsed her from a distance talking to the Vicar's son, Simon.

That evening, as the two girls were dressing for dinner, Louisa started to tease her.

"I fear he is not a suitable match for you, my dear friend. No high position and definitely no money."

"I know," Arabelle replied in a low voice.

"I only mention it because I know you believe marriage should be a sensible arrangement – why Arabelle, you're crying!"

"I can't help it," she choked. "We love each other so much, and there is no hope for us."

"You and Simon? Oh, Arabelle, tell me everything."

"We loved each other from the first moment. When we danced it was like being in a dream. I realise now that you are right. When you are in love, nothing else matters. But my parents want a rich man for me and I know they will refuse their consent.

"I used to want a rich man too." She began to laugh through her tears. "And my heart has chosen the poorest man in the world and I cannot live without him. Oh, Louisa, isn't that a horrible joke?"

They clung together, laughing and crying with joy and despair. Louisa felt closer to her friend than ever before, now that Arabelle also knew the joy of heavenly love and the dread that in the end she might be thwarted.

At last they walked down for dinner. It was a muted evening with just the four of them. Everyone was glad when Lady Hatton declared an early night.

When she was sure that her parents had retired to bed, Louisa threw on a cloak and hurried out to the stables.

No matter what Roderick said, she had to see him alone and in private. Being together out in the open where they needed to be careful of every word and action was no longer enough.

There was no sign of him in the stables, but she knew that he slept in the loft above. Climbing the ladder she found herself in a cramped, shabby room.

By the moonlight she could just make out a solitary table and chair, an old chest of drawers, with a plate and mug standing on it and a narrow iron bed that looked hard and uncomfortable.

Roderick lay there, his single blanket pulled tight around him in a vain attempt to ward off the cold. Louisa was ashamed, thinking of her own luxurious bedroom with its huge fireplace.

He must be exhausted, she thought, to have come to bed so early. While she had eaten in warmth and comfort, he had finished a hard day's work, eaten his frugal meal and collapsed into bed.

He was turned towards her and in the silver light from

70

the window she could see that sleep had wiped away all strain from his face, as he lay peaceful and untroubled.

Louisa dropped to her knees beside him and watched him with a kind of bittersweet joy. For this precious moment they were not lady and servant. She was simply a woman watching over a man who had seized possession of her heart. Whatever else happened, that would always be true.

'How can I love you?' she murmured. 'And yet – and yet – I do.'

It was the whisper of her breath against his cheek that woke him. He opened his eyes and found himself looking straight into hers.

He did not move for a long time and then said in a quiet voice,

"Are you really here or are you just another dream come to plague me?"

"I am really here. Don't you know it's me?"

"*Louisa* – ?" The word was very faint.

The next moment he reached for her and drew her close. Suddenly his lips were on hers in the kiss she had craved for. She was in his arms, feeling him hold her, knowing that for once he had no defences against her and nothing else mattered.

"Does a dream kiss like this?" she asked joyfully.

"Mine do," he sighed. "In my dreams you always kiss me."

"Was it like this – and this – and this?"

"Yes." He smiled, adoring her. "It was exactly like that. But when I awoke, I was always alone."

"You will never be alone again," she promised. "Not if you love me."

"I do love you. I have fought it as hard as I could, but I love you. I have no right to love you – but I cannot help myself."

Her heart bounded with joy. This was love as she had always dreamed of it. What did it matter that they would be poor as long as they were heart to heart and soul to soul?

But the next moment she felt him stiffen and he sat up in bed, fending her off.

"No," he groaned. "What am I doing? I swore I wouldn't."

"But it is all different now," Louisa cried passionately.

He took her shoulders. "If anyone found you here, the scandal could ruin you. You must go now. Turn away while I dress."

She ran to the window, almost weeping in her desperation and disappointment.

After a moment he said, "all right," and she turned to find him fully dressed.

He saw her distraught face and took her gently into his arms.

"It is so hard for you to understand, my love. To you the world is simple – we love each other and that is everything."

"But it should be everything," she claimed fervently. "You said you loved me."

"I do love you. How could I not, when you are so full of life and passion, so young and beautiful and when you honour me with your love – ?"

"Don't talk like a servant," she said fiercely. "You are more than that!"

"I do not say it as a servant, but as a man who is profoundly and humbly grateful for your gifts. If I was the Emperor of the whole world, I would still want to kneel before you in gratitude.

"One day, please God, I will be able to say these words

openly. But just now I must stay a servant with nothing to offer you."

"But when will our day come?" she pleaded.

She saw the sudden bleakness in his face and cried out,

"*No!* It must come. It *must*! Don't ask me to think of life without you."

"Try to trust me. There are things I must tell you – but not at this moment. It's too dangerous. Kiss me, my darling and then the dream is over for now."

"But not over for ever," she implored. "We will find a way."

"We will find a way," he agreed. "Kiss me."

They kissed each other again and again, until he said,

"I must take you back now, my darling, while I still have the strength to let you go."

As they walked back to the house a faint, beautiful sound reached them.

"It's the children," Louisa said. "They are singing carols."

They stood together in the starlit night, listening to the sweet young voices.

"They sound so pure and innocent," she mused. "If only they knew what the world is really like!"

Only a short time ago she had returned to England, thinking she was coming back to a happy place in a good world. Now she was beginning to understand the ugly side of life.

'But I will not be afraid,' she told herself.

She felt something fall softly onto her head.

"Snow," said Roderick. "The first snow of Christmas."

Louisa held out her hand and watched in wonder as the

snowflakes fell into it and vanished.

"You must go inside," Roderick told her. "You will catch cold."

"No, I want to stay a little longer. It is so lovely."

"Go indoors at once," he commanded quietly.

Louisa did so. It no longer felt strange to obey him.

CHAPTER FIVE

Soon the day dawned that Louisa dreaded, the day of the ball at Cranford Manor. Every night she had prayed that something would happen to save her from having to visit Lord Westbridge's home again.

She was more determined than ever to refuse him, but she could also sense the growing determination of her parents that she should accept his proposal.

But nothing happened to save her and on the evening of the ball, she submitted to being dressed under her mother's direction, in a gown finer than any she had ever worn.

It was made of pale blue satin, embroidered with silver stars. Silver slippers adorned her elegant feet and silver ribbon wound in and out of her bright curls. Around her neck she wore her family's pearls.

Lady Hatton was resplendent in a wine red dress. But Louisa frowned when she saw the garnets her mother was wearing.

"I think you should wear your rubies with that dress, Mama?"

"I cannot quite recall where I put them," Lady Hatton replied hastily.

"But surely, your maid – "

"My darling, what a fuss you make. Nobody will be

looking at me. All eyes will be on you. Hurry now. It is time to leave."

The carriage was waiting. Roderick ceremoniously opened the door and handed Lord and Lady Hatton in and then Arabelle. As Louisa reached out her hand to him, her cloak, which was lightly draped about her shoulders, slithered off.

Roderick picked it up and settled it about her again. He contrived to touch her as little as possible, but she was aware of the warmth of his hands, and when she looked at him she saw something in his eyes that made her heart beat faster.

It was a clear, brilliant night, cold but beautiful. The stars gleamed like diamonds in the sky and the moon flooded the snowy landscape with silver as they travelled the few miles to Cranford Manor.

And then there it was before her, the huge, luxurious house and they were drawing closer and closer. Lights blazed from every door and window and carriages swept up the drive in an endless stream, disgorging hundreds of guests.

"Everyone will be here," Lady Hatton said, awed. "Simply everyone."

The house glittered with Christmas decorations. The Great Hall was dominated by the biggest Christmas tree Louisa had ever seen. It reached up to the roof and was hung with tinsel and shining baubles. Presents were massed around the base.

Powdered footmen were everywhere, helping guests off with their cloaks. But Lord Westbridge himself took Louisa's cloak, contriving to allow his fingers to linger on her neck in a way that made her shudder.

"Now my house is perfect," he announced in his disagreeable voice. "You complete it."

"You are too kind, my Lord," Louisa responded in an unsteady voice. "Your house does not need me to make it perfect."

He took her hand. "My Lord?" he mocked. "How formal! I should prefer that you call me George – my most charming Louisa."

She raised her head and challenged him.

"I should prefer that you call me Miss Hatton."

He laughed. "How enchantingly old-fashioned. But I am not angry. I prefer you to have a sense of propriety – to begin with."

Her cheeks flamed at his words. But there was no way of escape. Her parents were looking on and smiling.

Other guests were looking too. All the most notable young ladies of the district regarded her with envy. They would have liked to receive attention from the wealthiest man in the County, and they thought how lucky she was.

But Louisa cared nothing for Lord Westbridge's wealth or his great house. Her thoughts were with Roderick. She had last seen him driving the carriage away after dropping them at the front door. Where was he now?

He had sworn to protect her, but there was nothing he could do against the powerful Lord Westbridge in his own house.

She began to feel that she had been very foolish to rely on Roderick. He would do his best, but a groom was helpless against a great Lord.

Guests were wandering around the huge rooms that had been newly restored and put on display. Wherever they walked, they gasped with wonder.

The great ballroom was a mass of holly, Christmas roses and pink silk hung in festoons. At the far end a large orchestra was tuning up. Clearly no expense had been spared.

It was time for the dancing to begin.

"May I have the honour of the first waltz?" Lord Westbridge asked Louisa.

His manner showed that he was confident of her acceptance.

Quietly she placed her hand in his and allowed him to lead her onto the dance floor.

"Permit me to tell you that you are the most beautiful woman here," he grated as they whirled about the floor.

"Thank you. But I wish you had not singled me out so obviously."

"Why not? Everyone here knows what I want from you – and so do you."

She wished he would not talk in such a manner. It was horrible being held in his arms.

"You hardly know me," she stammered. "We have met only twice."

"Once is enough. When I want something I don't shilly-shally. I want you and I am going to have you. Perhaps I will announce our engagement tonight."

"Without my consent?" she demanded, her eyes flashing.

"You are going to consent and we both know it. Otherwise – "

She did not allow him to finish.

"If you announce our engagement, I shall deny it and leave at once. That would make you look a fool."

Lord Westbridge's eyes blazed with anger.

"And if you did that, I would make you very sorry," he said harshly. "Very well. We will play the game out a little longer. It will make my revenge more enjoyable in the end!"

"Don't hold me so close," she begged.

"It pleases me to hold you close and I always do as I please. But the dance is now coming to an end."

He strolled away and for the next hour performed duty dances. Louisa tried to compose herself. Many men asked her to dance. She accepted although she did not really want to be with any of them. She wanted to dance with Roderick, the man she loved. But she was beginning to fear that her love was hopeless.

The Reverend Lightly and his family were present. Louisa watched as Simon and Arabelle greeted each other soberly for fear of betraying their secret.

But when they danced together their love seemed to flame from them, Louisa thought. She looked at her practical friend, who had judged marriage only by material standards. Now she too was ready to give up everything for love.

If you truly loved, that was how it changed you. Nothing else mattered in the whole world. And love would transform her life as it had transformed Arabelle's.

She danced until she was tired, longing for this night to be over.

If only she could tell her parents how improperly Lord Westbridge had spoken to her and trust them to put a stop to him. But she had come to realise that she could not rely on them for help.

At last there was a lull in the dancing. At Lord Westbridge's command everyone gathered around the great tree.

"There is a Christmas present for every one of my guests," he proclaimed.

Footmen began passing among them, handing out brightly coloured parcels. Louisa looked on as her parents opened their gifts.

For Lord Hatton there was a cigar box in solid gold.

Then Lady Hatton opened her gift and Louisa smothered a cry.

It was a jewel box. And inside it lay the ruby necklace that her mother had 'lost'.

It was as though a flash of lightning had lit up a nightmare landscape. The empty stables, the fewer servants, the missing jewellery. Her mother had been forced to sell her necklace and Lord Westbridge had tossed it back at her as a demonstration of his power.

"And now, my gift to you, Miss Hatton," Lord Westbridge declared.

He placed into her hands a large, flat jewel box. Louisa took it reluctantly. She would have liked to refuse, but she could not do so in front of so many people.

She opened it and found her worst fears realised. A huge, resplendent diamond necklace lay against the black velvet. It must have cost a King's ransom. There were gasps from the onlookers.

"I – I cannot accept this," she stammered. "It is far too costly."

Lord Westbridge shrugged.

"What is money when one pursues one's heart's desire. Accept this as a tribute of my devotion and esteem."

His words were humble, but the savage gleam in his eye told her that he was looking forward to the day when he could enforce his will upon her.

"Mama – " Louisa pleaded. "Papa – "

"A very nice little gift," her mother enthused. "Don't make a silly fuss, my dear. That would be ill-bred."

"And could I have the pleasure of seeing Miss Hatton wearing her necklace?" Lord Westbridge asked smoothly.

Lady Hatton removed Louisa's pearls and she stood there, feeling like a sacrificial lamb, as a fortune in diamonds was hung about her unwilling neck.

"There is a mirror in the next room," Lord Westbridge said. "Allow me to escort you and show you how magnificent you look."

He grasped her wrist and drew her towards the door. Louisa had no choice but to go with him.

When they were alone in the small ante-room, the girl in the mirror looked back at her from haunted eyes. Behind her stood Lord Westbridge, smiling a nasty little smile to himself.

"Thank you," Louisa said. "Now I think we should return to the others."

"Not so fast. I have lavished a fortune on you. Surely you can give me a few minutes of your time? I only want to show you some more of my house."

He drew her arm through his and led her out of the room by the far door.

"Did you know this used to be a monastery before it became a private house?" he asked.

"Yes," she whispered, half fainting.

"Of course the place is infested with tiny nooks and crannies, hiding places and secret stairs. There is even a ghost, which my valet swears he has seen."

"I – I have heard about the ghost," Louisa remarked. "It is supposed to be a headless monk."

"Headless maybe, but remarkably talkative, for all that. They say if he calls your name you go mad with fear. Just through here is the place where he is supposed to walk."

"Please I – I don't want to go any further."

"We are nearly there," he said, ignoring her.

He urged her through another door which he closed. He turned the key and leaned back against the door.

"Now we can have a little talk," he said.

"No, I want to return to my parents."

"You will leave when I say so. Nobody will be surprised that we have slipped away. Naturally a betrothed couple will want to be alone."

"But we are not betrothed," she cried.

"We will be when I have kept you here long enough, unless you want a scandal that you will never live down."

Louisa backed away from him. He was repellent.

She looked around wildly for a way of escape. But there was only one door and he was blocking it.

"No!" she screamed.

Lord Westbridge began to move towards her.

Horrified, Louisa saw the trap she had walked into. Why, oh, why had she let Lord Westbridge trick her into going alone with him? Now she was alone with him, ensnared. If he could keep her here long enough she would be forced to marry him.

"You did this on purpose," she screamed at him indignantly. "To compromise me."

"Let us say rather that I don't like wasting time. I am not going to be kept dangling by a chit of a girl. We both know what your answer has to be in the end."

"No! You cannot force me."

Louisa was backing away from him as she spoke. He advanced on her, grinning cruelly.

"I like a spirited filly," he snarled. "The more you fight, the more we will both enjoy the end."

"How can you want to marry me when you know I loathe you?" she cried.

"But my dear, stupid little girl, that is the best part. I knew you held me in aversion the first time we met. You tried to be polite, but it stood out on you like a halo." He laughed. "That was when I decided to have you."

"You – want me because I dislike you?" she stammered, scarcely ready to believe such perversity.

"Of course. Willing women are dead bores. Now you – you will never bore me because you will never be willing, but by God you will be submissive, madam, I promise you.

"You loathe me, but you won't be able to escape me. You may fight and struggle, but in the end, you will yield. You belong to me. You have belonged to me from the moment I decided to take you."

"I do not belong to you," she retorted with as much emphasis as she could manage. "And I never will!"

"Wonderful, wonderful! That's just what I like."

"You must be insane!"

His grin was horrible. "Let us just say I enjoy unusual tastes – which you can gratify like no other woman I have met. Now, we have talked long enough."

He reached for her. Louisa raised her arm to fend him off. He laughed and seized her wrist. Driven by fear, she performed the first unladylike action of her life.

Lord Westbridge yelled with pain as her teeth sank into his hand.

She took advantage of the distraction to dart past him, unlocking the door and fleeing through it. His bellow of rage only made her run faster.

She ran down a corridor, through a pair of double doors, then another and another. She had lost all sense of direction. She did not know where she was in the house or where she was heading. She only knew that she must escape from Lord Westbridge.

At last she stopped in a long, empty gallery. She listened intently for the sound of her tormentor following her, but all she could hear was the faint sound of music.

The gallery stood at right angles to the ballroom.

Through the windows Louisa could see the couples whirling in each other's arms and the orchestra playing vigorously. If only she could return to that brightly lit place, instead of here, alone and lost.

"*Louisa!*"

She almost screamed as she heard her name whispered from the darkness. She could see nobody, but again the sound came floating out from nowhere.

She remembered the story of the headless monk who whispered people's names, sending them mad with fear.

"*Louisa*," came the voice again.

"Who are you?" she cried. "Where are you? Oh, Heaven help me!"

"Hush, it's only me," whispered Roderick, appearing from the shadows. "Don't be frightened."

"Oh, Roderick!" she sobbed, flinging her arms around him. "Roderick, *Roderick!*"

He held her tightly.

"I slipped into the house by a side door and watched the ball from a gallery. When he took you aside I contrived to follow."

He laid his cheek against her bright hair.

"I promised you I would always be there, even when you couldn't see me," he said. "Did you think I had deserted you?"

"I don't think you will ever desert me," Louisa sighed.

But then she heard a sound that terrified her.

"He's coming," she murmured.

Roderick drew her far back into the shadows and they stood very still in each other's arms.

The door at the far end of the gallery was flung open and Lord Westbridge stood on the threshold. He was furiously angry.

"You cannot get away from me," he shouted. "Stop this nonsense at once."

Roderick's arms tightened around Louisa. She held her breath, feeling the beating of his heart against her own.

Lord Westbridge strode further into the gallery. For a terrible moment Louisa thought he would search the shadows. But at last he seemed to be convinced that she was not here.

"So you took the other way," he muttered. "Very well. I will find you there, then. And when I do, it will be the worse for you!"

He strode out the way he had entered, slamming the door behind him.

"You are safe now," Roderick said. "He thinks you have gone into the West wing. There is a maze of corridors there. He will be searching for a long time."

"He was trying to compromise me."

"I know. Give him time to move away and then you can slip back into the ballroom."

"People will have noticed that I was missing. They will think that he and I – oh, it's too horrible to think about!"

"Don't worry. I am going to take care of that."

"To think you were here in the gallery all the time, watching over me."

"I never took my eyes from you. You were the most beautiful woman in the room and you danced so gracefully."

"I didn't care for any of the men I danced with. I should have liked – " Louisa hesitated, before saying softly, "I should have liked to dance with you."

"I would have liked that too," Roderick admitted. "Every time a man put his arm about your waist I wished it was me – although I had no right even to think it."

Somehow his hand had crept about her waist. The

sound of a languorous waltz reached them from below. The next moment Louisa was swaying in his arms.

How had a groom learned to waltz so elegantly? His steps fitted perfectly with hers. He knew how to guide her gently but firmly. As they glided around the room together, Louisa felt as though she were dancing among the stars. She never wanted this beautiful moment to end.

Dancing with Roderick felt so right, as though he was the partner Heaven had ordained for her.

At last the dance came to an end.

"I will take you back now," he said dreamily.

"No," she begged. "One more dance. Just one more."

The music began again. Roderick held her close as they swayed together. Louisa never took her eyes from his face. She felt as if the walls and ceiling had dissolved. There was no reality but this moment and each other.

"Roderick," she whispered.

"I am here, my dearest. Never fear."

Her heart echoed the words, 'my dearest'.

He too, was her dearest. Here was the love she had longed for. There could never be another man for her but Roderick.

The music slowed and stopped. They never heard it. They were clasped in each other's arms.

Gently Roderick lowered his head and touched her lips with his. Louisa knew that this moment was what she had been waiting for all her life. The touch on her mouth was as light as a feather, yet it sent fierce, uncontrollable joy through her, as though every part of her heart, soul and spirit were coming alive for the first time.

All about her the world seemed to have stopped turning. Time and distance were nothing. There was only the beating of her heart. Only this man. This perfect love.

"We must leave here," he muttered unsteadily. "He must not find us together."

"I don't care if he does," Louisa exclaimed recklessly.

"My dearest love, I would not harm you with a scandal for anything in the world. Hurry now."

"But how can I return to the ballroom without him seeing me?"

"There are secret passages in this house he will know nothing about."

"But how do you – ? Oh, yes, you used to work here."

Roderick smiled.

"I know this house better than he ever will."

He drew her back into the shadows and lit a candle that stood on a low table. By its light Louisa saw him feel along the oak panelling until at last there was a click and a concealed door swung open.

She took his hand and he led her into the corridor.

It seemed they walked for ever. Roderick held the candle up to light the way, but all the passages looked the same to Louisa.

At last they found themselves facing another door. Roderick gently inched it open and looked out.

"This will bring you out near the ballroom. Go quickly while there's nobody about," he urged. "Try to join the crowd without being noticed."

"But what about Lord Westbridge."

Roderick grinned. In the flickering candlelight, it made his face look as mischievous as a schoolboy's.

"Leave that devil to me," he said. "I am going to teach him a lesson he will never forget."

As he had said, there was nobody about as she slipped out into the corridor. A large pair of double doors led to the ballroom. Louisa kept to one side and crept in, unnoticed by anyone.

She made her way to where her mother was sitting on a sofa by the wall with the other chaperones.

"There you are, my darling," Lady Hatton said. "But where is Lord Westbridge?"

"I do not know, Mama," Louisa replied with perfect truth. "I am afraid we became separated."

"But how could that happen?"

"This is a very large, confusing house."

A young man appeared and begged her for a dance.

"I think this dance was reserved for Lord Westbridge," Lady Hatton intervened quickly.

"But he isn't here, Mama."

Louisa took to the floor with her partner. The more people who saw her dancing the better. Then nobody could think that she was with Lord Westbridge in a scandalous *tête-à-tête*.

So after this partner she danced with another, and then another. Time passed and still there was no sign of Lord Westbridge.

What had Roderick meant when he spoke of teaching him a lesson he would never forget?

The guests began to express consternation that their host was absent for so long.

"Something terrible must have happened to him," said Lady Hatton. "He would not just go away and leave his own party."

Louisa was watching the powdered footman standing just inside the door. Another footman approached him from outside and muttered something in his ear. The men exchanged looks of concern.

"What has happened?" Lord Hatton demanded.

One of the footmen bowed.

"Somebody has heard a fearful noise upstairs," he said, "as though a man was trapped."

"We had better go and investigate," suggested Lord Hatton.

By now the other guests had realised that something was happening and they all thronged after the footman as they climbed the broad staircase.

Higher and higher they climbed, to the upper reaches of the house, where rebuilding was still continuing.

Now they could all hear the sound of hammering and shouting. It seemed to be coming from just inside a panelled wall.

"Hallo!" called the footman.

"Get me out!" came a muffled cry.

"But where are you, my Lord. I can see no door."

"Get me out of here, you fool!" Lord Westbridge screamed.

It took some time to release him, because the footman could not find the catch, and Lord Westbridge was too hysterical with rage to instruct him clearly.

But at last the secret door swung open and he emerged into the light of the room.

Now Louisa understood what Roderick had meant by a punishment he would never forget. Lord Westbridge was covered in dirt and cobwebs. Dust had ruined his magnificent clothes and fell from his hair into his eyes. When he tried to brush it away, he left streaks on his face.

All around him his guests were covering their mouths with their hands. Even so, some titters were clearly audible.

Lord Westbridge looked ready to do murder.

"My Lord," the footman gasped.

89

"Get out of my way, blockhead! What did you bring this crowd for?"

Lord Westbridge's cast his eyes over his guests until he came to Louisa, trying not to laugh. But he recognised that she had seen him looking ridiculous.

She thought that she had never seen so much concentrated hatred in one human face.

"It is getting late," Lady Hatton declared. "And time for us to be leaving."

She addressed Lord Westbridge graciously.

"Thank you so much for a delightful party."

The others found their tongues and uttered words of conventional civility, while their host stood there, looking like a chimney sweep and hating the lot of them.

Lady Hatton's good breeding sustained her until she was outside. Then she leaned heavily on her husband's arm.

"Such a terrible thing to have happened," she moaned. "Just when everything was going so well."

Roderick paused in the act of handing her into the coach.

"I trust your Ladyship is not feeling ill?" he asked.

"My Mama is suffering from strain," Louisa explained. "Poor Lord Westbridge was accidentally trapped in a secret cubby-hole."

Roderick's face was wooden.

"I grieve to hear it," he said. "I do hope his Lordship was not injured."

"Not at all. Just very dirty." Louisa met his eyes. "It was shocking!"

"As you say, miss."

All the way home Louisa and Arabelle tended to Lady Hatton.

"How could such an awful thing have happened?" she whined. "The poor man. So undignified!"

"It was, wasn't it?" Louisa agreed. "And the whole County there to see it. Use my smelling salts, Mama."

Lord Hatton was more robust.

"By Jove, he looked a sight! Wouldn't have missed it for the world."

"Frederick!" Lady Hatton snapped. "You are forgetting!"

"What? Eh? Oh, yes! "Well, my love. No harm done. After all, it wasn't Louisa's fault."

Louisa stayed with her mother until she reached her room and could be safely left in the hands of her maid. But as soon as she could, she slipped out of the house and ran to the stables.

"Oh, Roderick, how clever you are!" she cried. "However did you manage it?"

"It was easy. I threw my jacket over his head so that he could not recognise me and thrust him into that secret cupboard. I chose one at the top of the house, where it would be dirty and nobody would hear him.

"I left him there for an hour, then muttered something to a footman and slipped away. It serves him right for frightening you, my darling. I will never forgive him for that."

His voice grew quiet as he became entranced at the sight of her. She was standing in the lamplight, looking up at him, her eyes filled with love.

Louisa felt her whole soul reach out to him. She loved him. She did not care about the disparity of rank and fortune. There were no problems when love was strong and true.

"I have nothing to offer you," he murmured.

"Oh, Roderick, my dearest. Can you offer me your heart?"

"All of it. Forever."

"Then I want nothing else."

"But you don't know what you are saying. How can you live as the wife of a poor man?"

"Poor in money. Rich in love," she said recklessly. "My darling, I was brought up to be vain and foolish, like other girls. I thought I would marry a rich man with a title, because it was expected of me.

"I needed to discover love to know how little those baubles mean. If I have your love I have everything."

He stroked her face. His eyes shone into hers.

"We will be so happy in our cottage," she said eagerly. "I will learn to cook and do everything for you. Won't it be wonderful?"

"No," he said gravely. "I love you too much to ask such a sacrifice."

"Do not ask me to give you up," she cried passionately. "Now that we have found each other, we must always be together."

"And we will," he promised. "There has to be a way. Trust me, my darling."

"I will follow you to the ends of the earth," she vowed. "I do not care that you do not have a title. To me you are a Lord. Lord of my heart. And you always will be."

*

She managed to return to her room without being seen. Once there she threw herself onto the bed, luxuriating in her love.

'He is everything I have ever dreamed of in a man,' she told herself. 'And I shall love him for ever and ever.'

But then the thought of Lord Westbridge seemed to fall like a shadow over her joy. She remembered how angry he had been and how even her parents seemed afraid of him.

He would not give her up without a fight. The path of true love was strewn with pitfalls.

Who could tell what the future held?

CHAPTER SIX

Next morning Lady Hatton was in ecstasies over the diamond necklace.

"It's practically a declaration in itself," she sighed.

"Yes it is," Louisa retorted. "And that is why I don't want it. I tried to refuse it, Mama. Why didn't you help me?"

There was a passing look of unease on her mother's face before she recovered her poise enough to declare,

"Because I have your best interests at heart, my dear. I will not allow you to throw away your future on a moment's weakness. Now run back upstairs and dress properly."

"I am going riding, Mama."

"You are not. Lord Westbridge will almost certainly call this morning to make you a formal offer and you will be here to receive him."

"But Mama, I have already refused him."

"What!"

"Last night I told him I would not marry him. He cannot have misunderstood me."

"But you accepted his diamond necklace."

"I did not," Louisa replied desperately. "He forced it on me and I could not take it off before we left the house.

"If he calls this morning, please Mama, give it back to him and tell him I will not agree to be his wife. Say you refuse your consent."

"Your Papa and I have already given our consent."

"Without asking me?"

"You are too young to know what you want. We are doing only what is best for you."

In despair Louisa ran upstairs, where Arabelle helped her to dress in a morning gown of trimmed silk. Together they walked downstairs to await the dreaded arrival of Lord Westbridge.

Arabelle could not declare her true opinion in front of Lady Hatton, but secretly she sent Louisa many looks of secret sympathy.

As the morning wore on with no sign of Lord Westbridge, Lady Hatton grew increasingly edgy. Then she announced that he would certainly come in the afternoon and sent Louisa to change her clothes again.

But even this failed to produce the desired effect.

Lord Westbridge did not appear and by the end of the day both Louisa's parents were giving her dark looks.

"This is all your fault," her mother accused her. "Your behaviour last night disgusted him."

"If only I could believe that to be true, I would rejoice," Louisa cried rebelliously. "Now we can send the necklace back?"

"We shall do no such thing," Lady Hatton declared loftily. "We shall wait for him tomorrow. Where are you going?"

"To the stables. I haven't seen Firefly all day."

"You will remain here. I still have much to say to you."

Seeing that the others were too preoccupied to notice

her, Arabelle slipped discreetly away. A moment later she was creeping into the stables.

"The house is in uproar," she said when she saw Roderick. "They have been expecting Lord Westbridge all day, but he did not come. Louisa tried to escape to see you but they watch her like hawks."

"Thank you for telling me, miss. I don't think Westbridge will trouble us for a few days."

"Why, do you know something?"

"I have been in the village and there are plenty of rumours. A plain coach left Cranford Manor at first light with all the blinds pulled down."

"Would that man travel in a plain coach?" Arabelle mused.

"He would if he was hiding from the folk who had laughed at him. And rumour says his valet accompanied him."

"If only he may have gone forever!"

"That is too much to hope for. But it will be a few days at least before he can show his face in this district again."

"He was covered in cobwebs and dust," Arabelle said, laughing. "Everybody enjoyed it, for of all the people who were there last night, eating his food, drinking his drink, accepting his gifts, I don't believe there was one who actually likes him."

"He prefers to be feared than liked," Roderick said gravely. "How is Lou– Miss Hatton."

"It's all right, she has confided in me. She hates this man and will be overjoyed to know that she is safe for a while. Can I give her a message from you?"

"Just tell her that I love her. And here – " he took an envelope from his inner jacket. "This is for you. Mr. Simon Lightly gave it to me."

"Oh, thank you, thank you!" Arabelle kissed the letter in ecstasy and fled back to the house to share the good news with Louisa, who was so relieved that she managed to be quite cheerful over dinner.

Her parents congratulated themselves that she must be seeing sense at last.

*

Everyone was full of preparations for Christmas. People's faces wore smiles as the happy time approached and they found new warmth and charity in their hearts.

A huge Christmas tree was set up on the village green and hung with nuts and berries for the birds who found it so hard to scratch for food in winter.

From inside the Church, the choir could be constantly heard practising for the Carol service that would take place on Christmas Eve.

Like many ladies Louisa was eagerly helping to arrange the party for the poor children. There would be tea, cakes and jellies. A magician would perform tricks and every child would receive a gift.

As the days passed with no sign of Lord Westbridge's return, her spirits soared. Now she could briefly allow herself to forget that he threatened her happiness and indulge the luxury of her love.

Sometimes she and Roderick could snatch a sweet moment alone, but not too often, because he would not risk exposing her to gossip. So they had to make the most of occasions when they could be together in public. Luckily the Christmas preparations gave them several of these, not only for them but also for Arabelle and Simon.

One afternoon Roderick drove her and Arabelle into the village in a carriage piled high with presents for the party. Together they bore them into the hall and piled them around the tree.

The Vicar's wife was there with her family of daughters. They all laughed and chattered as they unpacked hampers of food.

They had baked a huge Christmas cake and they set it up in pride of place, surrounded by bowls of nuts and fruit, jellies and creams.

Then the doors were opened and the children poured in. Their faces were alight with excitement. Some of their parents were very poor and this party would be their only real Christmas pleasure.

At the height of the jollity, Santa appeared and boomed "Ho-Ho-Ho!" Louisa noticed that Roderick had vanished. A moment later her suspicions were confirmed when Santa winked at her.

She was moved almost to tears as she handed out gifts and saw the wonder in the children's eyes. There were dolls, teddy bears, wooden trains, boats, picture books. The air was loud with "oohs" and "aahs!"

When the gifts were all given out, Santa waved goodbye and vanished. A few moments later Roderick appeared.

"I am so glad you did that," Louisa whispered.

"Why, what happened while I was away?" he asked innocently.

They laughed together.

'Please,' she thought, 'let it always be like this, loving each other, happy just to be together.'

When every child had eaten his or her fill, the lights were dimmed until only a soft glow remained. The children gathered around the tree and began to sing carols.

Louisa was deeply affected as she heard the sweet young voices raised in celebration of the loveliest story in the world. A child, born in poverty, but destined to rule the world through love. In the first flush of her own true love, Louisa felt her heart swell with joy.

As she watched the innocent faces lifted to Heaven, she felt that anything was possible. Surely God would show the way for her and Roderick to be together!

When the party was over the children streamed out into the darkness, clutching their presents and chattering eagerly.

Roderick and Louisa slipped away to steal a few precious moments alone.

"I am so happy," she confided. "I never dreamed that love could feel so wonderful."

"Nor I. You are the first woman who has ever possessed my heart and you will be the last."

"I want to tell my parents. They will be shocked at first, but they will understand when they know that we mean everything to each other."

"Would you really marry a poor man and live without all the comforts you are used to?" he asked tenderly.

"If he was the man I loved, I would never be poor."

He seemed profoundly moved by her words. "And do you really love me as much as that?"

"I love you," she whispered, "*as much as that*."

He took her hand and pressed it against his cheek.

"I have something important to tell you, my dearest. I hope you will forgive me for deceiving you."

"You? Deceive me? I don't believe it."

"I am not who I pretend to be. My name is not Roderick Blake. It is Roderick Cranford. The old Earl, who used to own Cranford Manor, was my grandfather."

Louisa gasped in astonishment,

"Then *you* are the black sheep?"

"Yes, I am the black sheep," Roderick said, with a slight grin. "That day we met in the grounds at Cranford, I was there visiting my grandfather.

"As a boy I led such a riotous life that I was packed off into the Army. I liked being a soldier, but it meant I was far away, serving in India, when the old man needed help. I like to believe that I could have protected him from Lord Westbridge."

"Lord Westbridge? I don't understand."

"He ruined Grandfather. He cheated him out of every penny he had. When I heard the news I immediately resigned my commission and came home. I arrived in time to be with him at the end. He spent his last days living on the charity of friends and died a broken man."

"Then you – ?"

"Yes, I am the Earl of Cranford." He looked down ruefully at his rustic clothes. "The penniless Earl of Cranford, unless I can recover my inheritance. As my grandfather lay dying, I promised him that I would bring Westbridge to justice.

"I believe that promise gave him some comfort in his last moments. I intend to keep it. Westbridge has to be stopped. He has left a trail of ruin and despair wherever he has gone."

"It is as though a monster has come amongst us," Louisa said.

"Yes, he is a monster. He is insanely greedy and ambitious. He has always wanted a more important title. Being a mere Baron is not enough for him. He wants an Earldom at least.

"When he failed in that quest, he set himself to amass money by any means that he could, no matter how cruel or dishonest. His path is littered with broken lives."

"Oh, if only you can defeat him!" Louisa breathed.

"It is vital that I do. Only then can we be together."

"And we *must* be together for I will never love anyone but you."

"That is all I want to hear," he told her tenderly. "If only you knew what it has been like, pretending to be a servant and having to remain humbly in the background.

"I learned to endure it, but the worst torture was watching the woman I love hounded by that satyr, and being unable to do very much to protect her."

"Am I truly the woman you love?" she asked. "Let me hear you say it again."

"You are the woman I love and to whom I belong. One day – and please God it will be soon, I will say it to you every hour of every day, until you tire of hearing it!"

"You will wait until eternity for me to tire of your love," she responded tenderly. "Oh, my love – *wait*!"

"What is it?"

"I have just remembered what old Sal prophesied many years ago. I told you she said that when I first met my husband he would be wearing a mask.

"And you were. An Earl pretending to be a groom. That was your mask. And it means that everything is going to be all right."

"Yes, my darling. If we trust in God, everything will be all right."

All the way home Louisa was in a happy dream. Roderick loved her and somehow their marriage must be possible. When she told her parents the truth all obstacles would be removed.

But when she entered the house she received a terrible shock.

Her parents were waiting for her in the library. And so was Lord Westbridge.

He rose to his feet as she entered. His face was dark with annoyance.

"My darling, Lord Westbridge has been waiting for you," Lady Hatton twittered anxiously.

"Waiting for a very long time," Lord Westbridge said grimly.

"I have been helping with the children's party in the village."

"Which has been long finished. Your gardener's little girl returned home some time ago," Lord Westbridge countered.

"I am sorry. I did not know you were here."

"Lord Westbridge wishes to speak to you alone," her father said.

"No, please wait, Papa," Louisa answered quickly. "He can have nothing to say to me that you cannot hear."

"Your parents know what I have to say to you and have given their consent," Lord Westbridge intervened.

He made a slight jerk of his head towards the door. Lord and Lady Hatton departed at once.

Louisa gasped angrily. How dared this man order her parents about in their own home?

Just before he left, Lord Hatton took his daughter's arm and murmured,

"I do hope you will be reasonable." He slipped out of the room before she could reply.

Louisa faced Lord Westbridge, her head up.

"It is time to set our wedding day," he declared. "The sooner the better."

"I have not agreed to marry you," she retorted indignantly.

"Oh, you will marry me all right. That was decided as

102

soon as I saw you. I can take my pick of the girls in this County or any other. Wealth does bring its own advantages."

"Then take your pick of them, my Lord, and leave me alone."

"I have already told you, I want you. You please me. Your spirit pleases me." He smiled nastily and added, "and breaking it will please me even more."

There was something intimidating in his brutal assurance. It took all of Louisa's courage to assert,

"You are wasting your time, my Lord. I will not marry you."

She turned and walked out of the room. She was outwardly calm and dignified, but her heart was beating wildly.

She saw her parents standing in the door of the morning room. They had been waiting anxiously to hear what had happened. They read the truth in her pale, tense face.

"You have refused him," Lady Hatton moaned.

Louisa hurried into the morning room and spoke softly.

"Yes, I have refused him. I hate him. And Mama, Papa, I must tell you that I love another man."

"Nonsense," her father said. "You cannot throw away such a catch because of a piece of girlish nonsense."

"I have refused him," Louisa maintained, more firmly than she felt. "And that is the end of it."

To her alarm, her father turned pale and sat down heavily.

"My God, I am ruined," he wailed.

"*No*," Lady Hatton cried. "Louisa you must listen to your mother. Our fate lies in your hands."

"What do you mean, Mama? How are we ruined?"

"It was just an innocent little game of cards – " her father stammered.

At those words a chill of fear started in Louisa's stomach and rose, spreading all over her body. She tried to ignore it.

It was impossible – it *must* be impossible –

"But Papa – you gave up gambling." She could hardly speak.

"Your father has been gambling for many years," Lady Hatton stated bitterly. "Sometimes he lost, sometimes he won. But when he played with Lord Westbridge he always lost."

"Somehow it all mounted up," her father groaned.

"How much do you owe him?" Louisa asked, shaking.

"He can claim everything we own."

It was all becoming clear now – the dismissal of the stable hands, the sale of the horses. Above all she understood why she had been brought home early. Her parents had planned to sell her to Lord Westbridge!

She felt sick with horror.

"Mama," Louisa cried desperately, "please listen. I am in love with another man."

"But you don't know any other men," Lady Hatton said firmly.

"I love Roderick Blake," she proclaimed proudly.

"The *groom?*" Lady Hatton screamed.

"He isn't really a groom. He only pretends to be, because – he is really the Earl of Cranford."

"Don't be absurd," said Lady Hatton. "The Earl is an old man."

"No, he died. Roderick is his grandson. Lord Westbridge cheated him out of his inheritance, just as he cheated you, Papa."

"I recall he had the devil's own luck with cards," her father growled. "I thought it was uncanny at the time."

"You were certainly a poor loser," came Lord Westbridge's hated voice.

They all turned sharply. His Lordship had quietly entered the room. How long had he been standing there, listening?

Louisa faced him. "Roderick is here to bring you to justice," she challenged him defiantly. "And he will do it."

He gave an unpleasant, silent laugh. "You little fool! Roderick Blake is a scheming impostor, trying to step into a dead man's shoes. It's true that old Lord Cranford is dead, but so is his heir. The young Earl died in India, after a drunken brawl. Roderick Blake was his batman.

"India is far away and nobody has seen the young man for years. He must have thought he could get away with it. He manages to deceive credulous little girls with more imagination than sense, but he doesn't fool me."

Louisa flushed at the contemptuous way he referred to her.

"I don't believe you," she said firmly. "He is the true Earl and Cranford Manor belongs to him, because you cheated his grandfather out of it. Just as you cheated my father.

"Every penny you possess has been obtained by fraud and theft. But it's over. The Earl of Cranford has returned to bring you to justice."

His eyes narrowed. "When we are married, you will learn to mend your manners."

"I shall never marry you."

Lord Westbridge shrugged. He flung a cold glance at Lord and Lady Hatton.

"Talk some sense into her," he said and stalked out.

Louisa looked at her parents with horror and then fled upstairs. Her mother followed her. She was becoming hysterical.

"My child, you must heed your mother's pleas."

"Mama, I have always been a dutiful daughter, but this is wrong. I cannot marry one man while I love another."

"Don't speak of loving that impostor," Lady Hatton screamed. "You are not in your right senses."

"But I am. Oh, Mama, try to understand. *I am in love.* Truly in love for the first time in my life. Let me bring Roderick to you – "

"Never! Your father and I will protect you from that wicked man."

Lady Hatton dried her eyes and a stubborn look came over her tired face.

"I am acting in your own best interests, my child. One day you will appreciate that."

She swept from the room and Louisa heard the click of a key in the lock.

"Mama!" she cried.

She ran to the door and tugged at it, but it was firmly locked.

"Mama!"

She shouted and banged on the door, but there was no reply.

All she could hear was her mother's footsteps descending the stairs.

*

The next day Louisa was kept locked in her room. Her parents, who had once seemed so tender and indulgent, had become implacable.

Several times they came in to reason with her.

"If you do not marry Lord Westbridge, we are ruined," her mother claimed. "You would not want see your parents thrown out of their home?"

Louisa cast beseeching eyes on her father, who stood there looking uncomfortable. He had always doted on her. Surely he could not destroy her life in order to pay his gambling debts?

But looking into his face she realised that she no longer knew him. He was not a tower of strength, as she had always thought, but a rather weak man who could not accept responsibility for his actions. He would bully her into submission while pretending it was for her own good.

"Papa – " she pleaded, although knowing it was useless.

"I do not know what we did to deserve such an ungrateful daughter," he said to his wife, avoiding Louisa's eye. "She thinks of nothing but herself."

"Papa, don't do this to me, I beg you."

"I cannot stay here," he said hurriedly. "I hope that prayer and reflection will bring you to a sense of your duty."

He hurried out before he could hear more.

Her mother began to cry again

"We are ruined," she wailed. "What will become of us?"

"Mama," Louisa said desperately, "it was not me who ruined you. You want to pay Papa's debts with my life."

He mother's answer was a scream.

"May Heaven forgive you for saying such a wicked thing!"

Louisa had been raised as an obedient daughter. She began to believe that it was her duty to rescue them, even at the cost of the rest of her life.

But then she would think of Roderick, whom she

loved with a love that came from God. How could she leave him?

When this bitter choice racked her, she threw herself down on her bed and sobbed wildly with despair.

That night, as she lay staring into the darkness, thinking her life was over, she heard the key turn in the lock and sat up, fearing more tyranny.

But it was not her Mama who entered, but Arabelle. The two girls threw themselves into each other's arms.

"They have moved me to a room just down the corridor," Arabelle confided.

"How did you ever find the key?" Louisa asked.

"I used the key to the cellar door. It opens this room as well. One of the maids told me. The whole household is on your side."

"Is there any news of Roderick?"

"I spoke to him this afternoon. He is desperate. He said to tell you that he loves you and he will find a way to rescue you.

"He said too that if he can just collect the evidence he needs against Lord Westbridge, then your parents can be saved without your marriage. But you must hold out."

"If only," Louisa breathed longingly. "If only there could be a way out. I don't want my parents to suffer but I cannot – oh, Arabelle, I cannot leave Roderick."

"Of course you cannot leave him," Arabelle agreed.

"Tell him how much I love him."

Arabelle promised and slipped away. For another day and night Louisa was kept a prisoner, torn with indecision and misery. The next evening her mother came again to see her. She stayed only a few moments, just long enough to say,

"Lord Westbridge is coming to see you tomorrow and you will give him your consent."

She swept out without waiting for a reply.

Louisa knew that this was the end. One way or another she was to be forced to marry a man she loathed. The parents she thought had loved her would show her no mercy.

She waited for Arabelle to come to her, but tonight there was no sign of her friend.

'Has she too abandoned me?' Louisa wondered in despair.

Then, as she lay in total darkness, she heard a sound outside her room. The next moment there was a soft scratching noise as something was slipped under her door, and a soft rustle, like skirts.

Lighting a candle Louisa picked up the paper from the floor.

It read,

Be ready to leave at midnight.

"Oh, thank God!" she whispered fervently, throwing herself down on her knees. "I haven't been abandoned. There is still some hope."

By the candle's light she retrieved a small bag from the bottom of her wardrobe and packed into it a few necessities for travelling.

She selected her warmest winter clothes, but did not put them on until the last moment, fearful that her mother would come to see her and find her suspiciously dressed.

By midnight she was ready and sitting on her bed, anxiously waiting in the darkness.

Midnight. Twelve chimes from the Church clock in the village, floating over the snow laden fields in the clear air.

But nothing happened.

Nobody came.

Louisa sat there, motionless, while her heart filled once more with despair as the time passed. Next were the chimes for a quarter past twelve.

The shining hope had been dangled before her for such a brief time. Now it was snatched away again and the pain was sharper than if there had never been any hope.

Then she heard it.

The soft, almost inaudible sound of a key being turned in the lock.

The door opened a crack to admit someone.

"*Arabelle!*"

"Ssh! Are you ready to leave?"

"Yes, but what is happening?"

"There is no time to talk. You will soon understand. Come quickly."

She was in her night dress, with a cloak thrown over it, her dark hair hanging down around her shoulders.

She ushered Louisa out into the hall and locked the bedroom door behind her.

"The longer they think you are still in your room the better," Arabelle whispered.

Down through the silent house they crept, then across the hall and through the kitchens to the back door Louisa always used at night.

"Shall I go to the stables?" she asked.

But Arabelle shook her head as she opened the kitchen door.

"Head for that little copse over there," she said, pointing. "Luckily it's starting to snow again, so with any luck your footsteps will be hidden."

"What will you do?"

"Lock this door behind you and go back to bed. In the

morning I will be as astonished as anyone else to find you have gone."

Louisa hugged her. "My dearest friend. When will we meet again?"

"I don't know. God go with you."

Louisa hugged her again.

"And with you and may He send you such a friend to help bring your own love to happiness."

"Go now, quickly."

Louisa seized up her bag and began to hurry across the snow. Behind her she heard the door close and the bolts shot across.

Guided by the moonlight she reached the dark shape that she knew to be the copse. Then a hand seized her and she gasped.

"Hush," said Roderick's voice. "Not a word until we are safe."

Joyfully she followed his lead, her hand safe in his, until they reached the far side of the copse, where there was a rough road. There was a lantern, held up by a man she could not make out clearly and by its light she could see a shabby old dog cart.

"Why that's the Vicar's dog cart!" she exclaimed. Then she saw who the man was. "Simon!"

"Arabelle begged me to help you," he admitted with a grin. "I don't know what my father will say if he ever finds out. Still, it will be too late by then."

"Oh, you are so good and kind," she sighed, overwhelmed.

"Get into the back of the dog cart and hide under the blanket," Roderick told her. "Don't look out before I give you the word, whatever you do."

He helped her into the back and pulled the blanket

over her. Then he too climbed in, but sat on the side facing seat. She felt the bump and Simon climbed up behind the horse, heard him give the signal to start and they were away, swaying and jolting.

Under the blanket she sent a silent message to her parents.

'Forgive me, forgive me, but I *could* not do as you wish. It would have been death for me. Try not to hate me and I pray that we may meet again in happier times.'

It was a rough uncomfortable journey, but Louisa did not care. After a particularly sharp jolt she felt a large, masculine hand slip down between the folds of the blanket, and seized it between both hers.

She cared nothing for the discomfort. She had entrusted her fate to Roderick, the man she loved and would cling to all her days.

From now on nothing could go wrong.

CHAPTER SEVEN

Louisa lost track of time. She only knew that the journey seemed to go on for ever and then suddenly they stopped. Roderick pulled back the blanket.

"We are here, my dearest," he said, reaching out to help her down with both hands.

She was intolerably stiff and almost fell, clinging to him.

"Where are we?" she asked, looking around.

It was still totally dark, but from somewhere very close she heard the sound of a Church bell, striking one o'clock.

"We cannot have come very far," she said, puzzled.

"This is my father's Church in Lark Hatton," Simon said. "There's a curate's cottage here that is empty at the moment. Nobody will think of looking for you so close to home and you can hide here until the hue and cry dies down and I can move you on."

Through the trees they could see the imposing stone rectory, with one light still burning, despite the lateness of the hour.

"My father is sitting up late to write his Christmas sermon," confided Simon. "Follow me. This way."

The curate's house was right next to the Church. Simon let them in and lit a candle.

"I pulled all the curtains before I left," he said, leading them up the stairs. "Miss Hatton, I thought you would be best off in this room – " he opened a door, "because it cannot be seen from any other house. The window is small and looks directly onto the Church. Even so, you must be very, very careful.

"There is enough food in the house for several days and I will look in as often as I can."

"How long must we stay here?" Louisa asked.

"I am afraid you will be here alone," Roderick said. "I have to go back to Hatton Place and be found at my post in the morning. If I am missing too there will be a scandal and your name would be besmirched."

"But if we are going to be married – Roderick, let's marry at once, tonight!"

"I am afraid my father would not do so," Simon said. "He is a good man, but nervous and he fears Lord Westbridge. Now, I must try to return the dog cart quietly."

Impulsively Louisa kissed the young man on the cheek. "Thank you so much for helping us," she said. "I hope you don't get into trouble."

He chuckled. "I shall not mind if it makes Arabelle think well of me."

He gave them a cheeky wave and departed.

The next moment Louisa and Roderick were in each other's arms.

"I was afraid I would never see you again," he said hoarsely. "I felt so helpless – longing to protect you – "

"But you came for me," she cried joyfully, "and now we will always be together."

"Please God, we will – eventually."

"Must we wait to marry?" she asked him sadly.

"Just a little while. I cannot escape with you. If I run

now I lose my last chance to bring Westbridge to justice. And I must do that, for us, for your parents, for all the others he has ruined and for my grandfather whose only peace at the end came from my promise to avenge him."

She wanted to cry out and protest that they should grasp their chance of happiness now. But she knew it would be useless.

Roderick was an honest man, inflexible in his decision to do what was right, at whatever cost of pain and hardship. And while she ached for the chance they might lose, her heart honoured him.

Instinctively she had chosen a man she could admire as well as love and though it tortured her, she would force herself to be as courageous as he.

"Yes, my love," she said. "You have a duty to do first. And then it will be our time."

He seized her in a clasp of fierce thankfulness.

"Thank you!" he exclaimed. "It would have been so hard if you had not understood."

"But shall we be apart for long?" she enquired sadly.

"I do not know. I am doing all I can to bring that man to justice, but it isn't easy. He has protected himself so well and his very name brings fear. The most important move was to spirit you away before you could be forced into marriage with that monster. Simon has friends in the next County who can hide you – "

"The next County," she echoed in horror. "So far away? Will we ever see each other?"

"I fear not. But he will be our go-between, and somehow we will manage to stay in touch."

She looked at the vista before her and separation from the man she adored, without knowing how long it might be and she shuddered. Only the deepest, most devoted love could help her endure it.

But they loved each other. And with God's help they would be strong enough for anything.

Roderick took her face between his hands, looked at her for a long moment before lowering his head and laying his lips on hers. Louisa felt herself transported to Heaven by the loving gentleness of his kiss.

This was the love she had dreamed about, passionate and steadfast. Whatever the future might hold, she knew this wonderful love would endure to the ends of their lives and beyond.

Whatever the future might hold, she would cherish this moment for ever.

Roderick raised his head and spoke very quietly and seriously.

"You are my own true love, in this life and into the next. And I want you to know that in my heart you are already my wife, now and forever. There can be no other."

"My husband," she whispered. "Lord of my heart."

She pulled back the curtain over the little window. In the moonlight they could make out the Church close by, towering above them.

"The day will come," he said "when we stand before the altar in that Church and become one in the sight of God."

"Roderick – let us do it now."

"My darling, Simon explained – "

"No, not with the Vicar. We don't need a Vicar, just us pledging ourselves to each other in the sight of God. And then, however long we have to be apart, we will know that we are truly married."

"You are so right, my love. But can we get into the Church?"

"The Reverend Lightly never locks it. He says people should be able to enter a Church at any time."

They slipped out of the little cottage into the cold night air and made their way across the snow to the porch. The door creaked but opened easily and they were inside the Church.

From the faint moonlight coming through the stained glass windows they could just make out the gleam of candlesticks on the altar. Slowly they approached the altar rail and knelt side by side.

"If the Vicar was here," Roderick said, "he would ask me if I would love you, comfort you, honour and keep you, in sickness and in health, forsaking all others, as long as we both shall live. To all these, I say yes, with all my heart."

"And I promise," Louisa breathed fervently, "to love and honour you, obey and serve you, and keep you in sickness and in health, forsaking all others, as long as we both shall live."

Roderick took her hand between his and began to speak.

"I, Roderick, take thee, Louisa, to my wedded wife, to have and to hold, from this day forward, for better or worse, for richer or poorer, in sickness and in health, to love and to cherish until death us do part."

Tears of joy had overtaken Louisa, but she managed to say her part, looking deeply into his eyes and speaking huskily.

"I, Louisa, take thee Roderick, to my wedded husband – "

While she spoke he regarded her with a look of unutterable love.

When he vowed to endow her with all his worldly goods, she smiled. They possessed no worldly goods between them, none at all.

And yet they had everything.

They had the whole world and Heaven too.

They walked silently back to the house, arms entwined and climbed the stairs together. In the tiny, shabby room they clung to each other.

"I must go soon," he muttered against her hair.

"I know. I hate to think of you walking all the way back. Go, my love – my husband. And yet – one kiss – one kiss – "

He kissed her repeatedly. They both knew the parting was inevitable, yet neither could bear to break away.

"My love," he sighed, "dearer to me than my life, I shall be with you soon. One day this will seem like a dream."

"My husband," she murmured. "Whenever you come to me, you will find me waiting for you."

"One last kiss – "

He laid his lips on hers in a gesture that was both a farewell and a promise. For a long moment they stood there, their hearts beating as one, knowing the true joy of love given and received equally.

And then, in a few brutal moments, it was all snatched away.

There was an ominous sound downstairs, footsteps rapidly climbing.

The door was kicked violently open.

There stood Lord Westbridge. And on his face a sneer of pleasure so vile that Louisa shuddered.

The next moment he stood aside, revealing three thick-set ruffians. Louisa screamed as they rushed into the room and hurled themselves savagely on Roderick.

He fought them as long as he could, but he was no match for three of them and soon they had forced him to the ground, where they could kick him. Lord Westbridge seized

Louisa, holding her in a grip of iron, forcing her to watch.

"No," she screamed. *"No, no – stop, don't hurt him!"*

But her words were not heeded. The three men continued their vicious work until Roderick lay unconscious on the floor. Louisa fought madly, but Lord Westbridge's grip was ruthless.

"How foolish of you to think you could escape from me. Luckily you were seen running from the house by a man who was on your land that night to do a little poaching. He knew I would pay well for the information.

"I would have caught up with you earlier but the man lost sight of you. I wonder how you knew to come here."

"I was told this house was empty," she replied quickly, fearful of getting the Lightlys into trouble. "It's common knowledge. I took a chance on getting in."

"For the Vicar's sake I hope that's true. You three, why are you just standing there? I didn't tell you to stop."

The three men had paused over Roderick's broken, bleeding body."

"Oh, God," Louisa wept, "you've killed him."

"He had better not be dead," Lord Westbridge snapped.

One of the ruffians checked.

"No, My Lord."

"Good, because I have further pleasures for him."

"No, no, *no* – " Louisa wept.

Lord Westbridge shook her.

"You have the audacity to weep for him in front of me? That is one more offence for which you will have to suffer. Not now, but after our marriage, when you will be my property and nobody can gainsay me. Now, be silent, you are beginning to annoy me. *Be silent I say."*

Louisa was in a state of collapse, incapable of anything more than a soft moan. If he had not been holding her tightly she would have crumpled like a rag doll.

"Take him out of here," Lord Westbridge snarled. "There, enjoy your last look at him, my Lady. You will never see him again in this life!"

Through streaming eyes she watched as the men lifted Roderick and carried him out of the room. Lord Westbridge was holding her back against him with one arm across the front of her shoulders. His other hand had vanished. He seemed to be reaching for something.

Suddenly his hand reappeared, holding a cloth. She had only one second to realise what was happening before the cloth was clamped across her face. She tried to struggle but it was useless against the ominous vapour of chloroform that filled her nostrils and infused her brain. She slumped unconscious.

*

Everything swam before her, furniture blending into wallpaper, faces coming and going. After a while things settled into place and Louisa realised that she was back in her own room.

She fought for her memory, but her last sight had been of Roderick's unconscious body being hauled away. Then Lord Westbridge had contrived to overcome her with chloroform, and now she was at home. But everything that had happened in between was a blank.

She became aware that she was not alone. Her mother's tear stained face hovered over her.

"Oh, my darling, you are awake at last. We thought you were dead. When we heard about the terrible thing that happened to you, we had such fears – "

"What – terrible thing, Mama?"

"Oh, Heavens, your mind is wandering."

"No, my dear," that was her father, appearing beside the bed. "After her dreadful ordeal it is only natural that she should be a little vague."

"What – happened?" Louisa asked hoarsely.

"That wicked man abducted you. It is only thanks to Lord Westbridge that you were saved."

"He – didn't – abduct me – "

Lady Hatton gave a little scream and hurriedly put her hand over her daughter's mouth.

"Yes, yes he did, my darling. He snatched you against your will – "

"No – " Louisa cried frantically, "I went with him – gladly – "

"Do not try to shield him," her father interrupted. "It is like you to be generous, but Lord Westbridge told us how he found you struggling in that fiend's arms, screaming for help."

"You are so fortunate in Lord Westbridge," her Mama chimed in eagerly. "Even after finding you in such a – compromising situation, he is *still* willing to marry you."

"Marry – him?"

"For pity's sake Louisa, this is your last chance of a husband."

"Never," she muttered weakly. "*Never*."

"Your pardon, madam, if I could just have a word with your daughter."

Lord Westbridge stood in the doorway, his face a mask of sympathy. But she could see through it to the devil beneath.

"Yes," Louisa said quietly. "I want to talk to him alone."

She kept her eyes fixed on Lord Westbridge as her parents left the room. Suddenly she was filled with cool determination.

"Where is he?" she whispered hoarsely. "You devil! What have you done with him?"

"He is a madman. His fantasies were becoming dangerous. I have had him placed under restraint."

"You mean – ?"

"There is a most efficient lunatic asylum in town. He will be well looked after, until his – er – delusions – are cured."

Louisa covered her eyes. It was too horrible to contemplate.

"You cannot do such a wicked thing," she sobbed.

"Wicked? I am merely taking care of him, to ensure that no harm comes to him. His incarceration may be a short one. *Or it may be a very long one.*"

With a sudden harsh change of tone he seized her, pulling her hands away from her face and forcing her to look at him.

"This nonsense has gone on long enough," he snapped. "We are announcing our engagement today."

"No!" she cried.

"Don't you understand that you have no choice? Think of your parents. Think of Roderick Blake."

"And if I marry you – ?" she asked desperately.

"That will make matters easier – for everyone."

It was as he had said. She had no choice. The face looming above her was implacable. In despair and heartbreak, Louisa mumbled,

"Very well, Lord Westbridge. I will marry you."

*

The district was agog with excitement. The engagement had been announced of Lord Westbridge to Miss Louisa Hatton and the wedding would take place almost immediately.

Louisa knew that everyone thought she must be the happiest girl in the world and it only added to her misery.

Again and again she relived the magical moments when she had knelt beside Roderick in the sight of God, and they had been married in their hearts.

Many times she hovered on the verge of telling her parents about her 'marriage', but she knew it was useless. They would not believe her and if they repeated her words to Lord Westbridge, he might have Roderick killed.

That was the terror that kept her silent.

There was only one person in whom she could confide and it was Arabelle. Gradually she discovered that her friend had played her part perfectly, seeming to sleep late the next morning and be awoken by the sound of the house in uproar over Louisa's disappearance.

"Then I threw a fit of hysterics," she told Louisa with grim humour. "I thought if I was screaming they could not ask me any awkward questions."

"You have been wonderfully clever," Louisa said.

"Clever enough to abuse you a little. Your parents think I am shocked by what you did, and rely on me to preach submission and obedience to you. Otherwise they might keep me from you. As it is, I may still be of some help."

Louisa squeezed Arabelle's hand. It was wonderful to have such a friend, but even so, what could she do? The future still looked bleak and hideous.

"Did the Lightlys fall into any trouble?" she asked, fearful of the answer.

Arabelle shook her head in reassurance.

"Lord Westbridge never pursued them. If he had made a fuss, it would have revealed to the world that his chosen bride had fled from him with another man, and that would wound his pride."

*

Lord Westbridge seemed determined to put her on display as he would have exhibited a beautiful vase that he had bought at a great price. He presented Louisa with a diamond ring so large that she flinched away.

"It – it will weigh my hand down," she objected.

"It will proclaim to the world that you belong to me," Lord Westbridge informed her coolly.

"But I am a person, *not* a possession," she cried. "Even when we are married – "

"You will belong to me," he broke in with a voice of iron. "My wife is mine as my house is mine and my furniture is mine. And like all my possessions, she must be a credit to me!"

Louisa shuddered.

"Incidentally," he added, "I have not yet asked you exactly what occurred between you and that madman – "

"Nothing," she replied quickly. "Nothing at all."

At all costs Roderick must be protected.

Her denial made no impression on this snake-like man.

"As I was saying, before you were so impertinent as to interrupt me," he resumed coldly, "I have not yet demanded the full truth from you. I am saving that pleasure until our wedding night."

"But I have just told you," she cried desperately. "Nothing – "

"Be silent. When I want to know, I shall inform you

of the fact."

He seemed bent on wiping out all traces of her previous life. She would no longer be allowed to ride her beloved Firefly. Lord Westbridge gave her a new mare. Although beautiful, she was too placid for Louisa. But he insisted.

"My dignity demands that you behave with decorum," he proclaimed coldly. "I will not allow you to racket around the countryside as you have done in the past."

She could not hope for any help from her parents. Lord and Lady Hatton were so thankful to be relieved of their money worries that they could think of nothing else. They blinded themselves to their daughter's torment and tried to believe that all was for the best.

Louisa felt as though she had never really known her father and mother. She had believed that they loved her. But now they were ready to sacrifice her.

"How can you be so ungrateful?" Lady Hatton admonished her. "Not every man would have overlooked your unfortunate involvement with a groom.

"But your future husband is most generous. Look at the jewels he showers on you. Not just the ring, but the sapphire and diamond tiara, the emerald necklace. The set of pearls he sent for you to wear at the wedding is worth a King's ransom."

"I cannot even choose anything for my own wedding," Louisa screamed. "He is actually paying for my dress."

"We could hardly have afforded a dress luxurious enough to suit him."

"But Mama, it is so vulgar. He only wants to show off his wealth."

Lady Hatton gave a little shout.

"I beg you not to say such things to him. It would be

most improper of you to dispute with your husband. He will be your Lord and Master. It will be your duty to obey him in everything."

"Very true," agreed Lord Westbridge, who had entered the room just in time to hear their conversation. "I have come to take you riding, my dear."

"I – I have a headache," Louisa faltered.

"Obey me," he said softly.

Reluctantly she did so. It broke her heart to ride with the man she detested after the wonderful rides she had shared with the man she loved.

*

She grew more and more heavy-hearted as the net tightened around her.

At night she cried herself to sleep.

Roderick haunted her dreams. What was happening to him? How badly did he suffer? Did he think she had betrayed him? Would she ever see him again?

One afternoon she was sitting at the piano playing soft, mournful chords, when Arabelle came hurrying in, looking around for any sign of Lord and Lady Hatton.

"I am alone," Louisa said. "What is it?"

Arabelle came to sit beside her and spoke softly.

"Go to the empty cottage on the other side of the stream," she whispered. "Hurry. I will go on playing and they will think it is you."

Louisa's heart beat with a mixture of fear and anticipation. Darkness was falling and she ran until she reached the cottage.

There were no lights and the place seemed empty. She stepped inside and stood while her eyes grew accustomed to the gloom.

Then she heard a groan.

"*Roderick!*" she whispered in disbelieving joy.

At last she saw him, lying on a bed in the corner, his hands reaching out to her. She threw herself down beside him, crying,

"Oh, my darling. Thank God! Thank God! Where have you been?"

"That devil had me locked up as a madman," he told her hoarsely. "I managed to escape and reach here."

To her horror she found that he was badly hurt. His body was covered with cuts and bruises and there was a wound to his head.

"What have they done to you?" she wept.

"It is a – bad place," he whispered. "But never mind now. Someone helped me to break out."

"Lord Westbridge claimed that you are an impostor and that the real Earl died in India."

"Do you believe that?"

Her beautiful, innocent eyes glowed.

"My love, I know you are the soul of truth and honour. I never doubted you for a moment."

"God bless you," he murmured."They will be looking for me. I should not have come here – putting you in danger – but the curate's cottage isn't safe any more, and you are the only home I know now."

"Of course you came to me," she exclaimed passionately. "Who should care for you but me?"

"Just until – I am strong enough to leave."

"And then we will leave together. I will follow you to the ends of the earth."

"Such a beautiful dream. But my darling, we must wait a little longer. Westbridge has claimed so many victims and now I may have found the way to save them."

"But how?"

He was seized by a coughing fit. When it was over, he was exhausted.

"I will tell you when I am stronger."

"Roderick, I must tell you something – "

"I know. You are betrothed to Westbridge. Word reached me in the asylum. I suspect that he arranged that it should. That fiend enjoys the thought of driving me mad."

"But you must understand that I only did it for your sake. He had imprisoned you in that dreadful place – "

He gave her a weak smile, full of love and trust. "My dearest, do you think you have to explain to me? I realised at once why you had agreed to him."

"But he has set the wedding date for next week. I couldn't stop him. What can we do?"

"Act as if all is well. Do not arouse his suspicions. I need a little more time. Trust me. I will save you."

"Don't allow me to be forced to marry him," Louisa implored.

"You are my wife forever," he reminded her.

Then a shudder overtook him and he closed his eyes.

She sped back to the house and slipped inside. Arabelle was still doggedly playing the piano. She looked up with relief when Louisa returned.

Hurriedly Louisa explained what she needed, and together they ran to the kitchen, which was quiet at that time of day. Together they packed a basket of food and wine. From her bedroom Arabelle fetched an old petticoat.

Louisa's heart was beating madly as she crept down through the dark house. At any moment she expected someone to stop her. But she was largely safe from being watched because Arabelle was playing the role of '*dragon*' so effectively.

Lord and Lady Hatton entrusted her with the task, not knowing that Arabelle was heart and soul on their daughter's side. So Louisa slipped out of the house without trouble.

She found Roderick sitting up, although still very weak. She gave him some wine and food and while he was eating she fetched some water from the stream that flowed outside. Then she tore the old petticoat into strips. She used some of them to bathe his wounds and some to dress them.

"My angel," he sighed, smiling.

It felt sweet to look after him. All around them lay disaster, but just for a little while she could pretend that she was his wife. It was the most beautiful moment of her life.

"When we are old we will look back on this time and smile," she said eagerly.

"Oh, Roderick, we will grow old together, won't we? God could not be so cruel as to part us when we have just found each other?"

"We will be together," he said weakly. "We will teach the world what a happy marriage should be."

"Promise that you will love me always, as I will love you."

"I will love you always," he vowed. "I will never love any woman but you. Whatever happens, you will live in my heart as the perfection of womanhood."

She kissed him, moving gently so as not to hurt his wounds. To her this kiss was a sacred act. With it she consecrated herself to Roderick again, heart and soul, as she had done at the altar in the Church. And she knew it was the same with him.

"You must go now," Roderick said at last.

"I cannot leave you," she protested.

"You must. It's dangerous for you to be here."

"I will come back as soon as I can."

"Take care of yourself, my darling," he urged softly.

"I will be back tomorrow."

"Not during the day. It's too dangerous."

Somehow she endured the following day. She rode again with Lord Westbridge and managed to smile. That night he came to dinner and she forced herself to be charming.

Once she looked up and found him regarding her out of narrowed eyes. But he said nothing.

Late that night she slipped out again. She found Roderick on his feet, but almost at once he swayed and she helped him back to bed.

"There isn't much time," he grunted. "There is something you must do tomorrow."

"Anything," she said fervently.

"Go and see Lord Westbridge. Go to the house. Try to find one of the maids, called Jenny. Give her this."

He handed her a sealed envelope. There was nothing written on the outside.

"But who is she? How can Jenny help us?"

"She is the – what was that?"

They both froze, listening.

"I heard a noise," he muttered.

Louisa ran to the window and looked out anxiously. But she could see no sign of movement.

"Be gone quickly," Roderick told her.

His arms encircled her and he drew her close.

"One last kiss," he whispered.

"No, not the last," Louisa said frantically. "It must not be the last. We must find a way to be together."

"I pray to God that we do."

He kissed her again.

"But if anything should happen, my darling," he said, "you will remember always how much I loved you."

"Do not talk like that. Nothing will go wrong. Oh, my love, my love!"

"Go now," he said urgently. "And pray we meet again."

CHAPTER EIGHT

The next morning Louisa dressed in her most attractive riding habit and she and Arabelle rode over to Cranford Manor. She greeted Lord Westbridge with a smile.

It went so much against the grain, but it was for Roderick, for their love and the hope of a future together.

"I hope you don't mind my calling unexpectedly," she said. "I wanted to look over my future home."

"It is always a pleasure to see you," he replied.

But his eyes were sharp and suspicious.

Louisa did not notice. She was working hard to keep her promise to Roderick. She assumed a slightly lofty air.

"If I am going to be Mistress of the house, I should meet my future staff."

"Very well. I will have them lined up for you."

Within a few minutes all the servants in the house had assembled in the hall. Lord Westbridge took her slowly along the line.

"This is Mrs. Jenkins, the housekeeper, Hepworth the butler, the chief parlour maid – "

It seemed endless. Louisa began to fear that she would never reach Jenny, but at last they reached a girl who looked rather vague and stupid.

"What do you do, Jenny?" Louisa asked kindly.

"I'm a maid, miss?"

"Yes, but what do you actually do?"

"Beg pardon, miss?"

Louisa's heart sank. How could this be the saviour who would help them overcome the frightful Lord Westbridge?

"My Lord!"

Louisa turned to see who had spoken. The man who stood there was dressed all in black. He was small, thin and looked like a weasel. There was something mean and unpleasant about his face and Louisa shuddered.

"This is Compton, my secretary," Lord Westbridge said. "I did not include him in the line because he deals only with my very private affairs. What is it, Compton?"

"Someone to see you, my Lord. Very urgent."

"Very well. You may all go."

Lord Westbridge snapped his fingers and the servants began to disperse.

Louisa seized her chance.

"Jenny," she said, "have you ever thought of becoming a lady's maid?"

"Me, miss? Oh, no, miss."

The others were disappearing. Soon she would be alone with Jenny. She struggled to keep the conversation going.

"Would you not like to learn how to dress my hair and keep my clothes?"

Jenny thought for a long time.

"I just fetch the coal, miss."

Louisa took the envelope from her reticule.

"Take this," she whispered urgently.

Jenny looked puzzled, but she slipped the envelope

into her pocket. A terrible thought occurred to Louisa. Suppose there was another Jenny? How could this stupid creature be the right person?

She was sure she had made a ghastly mistake.

Then she looked up and her heart nearly failed her.

Compton, the secretary, was standing there. He was watching her from eyes that looked like flints. He had seen everything.

Jenny scuttled away. Louisa felt faint. She had failed. She was sure of it.

"Shall I have some tea brought to you, Miss Hatton?" Compton asked.

"No, thank you. Since Lord Westbridge is busy, I shall leave."

She hurried away. She longed to run straight to the cottage to see Roderick, but she did not dare.

Darkness must fall before it would be safe.

She spent the rest of the day discussing wedding preparations with her mother. All the time she was thinking of a very different future.

But later that afternoon, disaster struck.

A maid summoned Louisa downstairs. She descended, full of foreboding, to find Lord Westbridge in the library with her parents.

Lady Hatton was saying something to him in a trembling voice. But his face was black with fury.

"I have not come here for social niceties," he snarled. "I have come, madam, to tell you that your daughter has been behaving disgracefully. Roderick Blake escaped from the care in which I placed him. In defiance of my express wishes she has been hiding him."

"I do not believe it," Lord Hatton tried to defend his daughter.

"Then you will experience quite a shock when you see the evidence," Lord Westbridge snapped. "He is in the cottage on the far side of the stream that runs through your property."

His accurate knowledge made Louisa gasp with horror. Lord Westbridge grinned. He moved close to Louisa and stood looking down at her.

"You thought you were so clever, but you gave yourself away."

"How?" she asked, trembling.

"By being nice to me, of course! I became suspicious as soon as you smiled at me."

He seized her wrist with cruel fingers.

"Now we will go and find Roderick Blake and you can witness his fate for yourself."

He strode from the room, dragging Louisa after him. She struggled but his grip was implacable. Lord and Lady Hatton followed, pleading and protesting uselessly.

Outside Louisa found two large men in white coats.

"They are the guards from the asylum," Lord Westbridge grated. "They will take him back where he belongs and keep him there."

"*No*," Louisa screamed. "No, please don't hurt him."

Lord Westbridge never heard her. He was heading for the little cottage where she had thought that Roderick could be safe. Tears poured down her face.

The cottage came into sight. Nearer and nearer he dragged Louisa until at last they were facing the door. Lord Westbridge kicked it in and strode inside.

Then he froze in his tracks. Everyone else came to a halt behind him.

The cottage was empty. There was no sign of Roderick.

Louisa squealed with hysterical laughter. Roderick had escaped. Lord Westbridge's furious face showed that he realised it too.

"Get after him!" he bawled at the two guards.

They ran out, but stood looking out over the countryside. Baffled. The snow had melted and there were no tracks to help them.

"No matter," Lord Westbridge growled. "We will find him sooner or later."

Louisa's laughter faded, to be replaced by a return to despair. Roderick had escaped but he was too weak to go far. Whatever he had planned to do about Lord Westbridge would have to be abandoned. Their last hope was gone.

"Take your daughter home," Lord Westbridge ordered Lord and Lady Hatton. "And make sure she behaves herself until our wedding day."

"She will be locked in her room," Lady Hatton promised.

Louisa faced her husband to be.

"I despise and detest you," she hissed in a low voice. "And if I have to marry you, I will make you rue the day."

Lord Westbridge's eyes gleamed.

"That's the spirit," he gloated.

*

The week before Christmas was set for Louisa's wedding day. It should have been the happiest of her life, the day on which she united herself with the man she loved.

But her true love was far away. She knew not where. It was to be the one man she hated who would wait for her at the altar.

On the night before her wedding Louisa stood at her window looking out on the silent countryside and spoke to Roderick in her heart.

'My dearest, I don't know where you are, or whether I will ever see you again. But even if I do, it will be too late after tomorrow.

'I want you to know that you are my true husband and will be forever – all my life, until the day comes when we can be joined in Heaven. My heart is yours and my life is yours, although the world will see me as the wife of another man.

'Until my last moment I shall belong to you – and love you.'

Then her heart broke and she let out an anguished cry.

"Where are you? Come to me! Come to me!"

But there was only silence. In the distant countryside nothing stirred.

Clear across the land she heard the chimes of the Church bell, the same bell that had swung above them when they claimed each other in marriage.

As it reached the last stroke, she fell on her knees beside the window in a passion of weeping.

After a moment Arabelle came and knelt beside her, taking her in her arms. They stayed together for the rest of the night.

*

Next morning Louisa rose, stiff and cold, but bleakly resolute. Whatever the day might hold, she would have courage.

She shuddered as she donned the showy, luxurious dress Lord Westbridge had demanded. It was made of yards and yards of heavy white satin, encrusted with real pearls. The long, flowing veil was antique lace, held in place by a diamond tiara.

More diamonds hung about her neck, seeming to choke her. And yet more weighed down her wrists and hands. She would have liked to sink from shame.

Lady Hatton swept into the room. She was resplendent in furs and velvet, but she could not meet her daughter's eye.

"The carriage is here, my darling. Your Papa is waiting below."

"Then let us be going, Mama," Louisa agreed tonelessly.

In too short a time she was aboard the family carriage, being borne to her wedding. It was to be held in the private Chapel that belonged to Cranford Manor. For this Louisa was thankful. If it had been held in the same Church where she and Roderick had claimed each other in marriage, she would not have known how to bear it.

A group of tenants was waiting outside when they arrived. They waved and cheered as she descended from the carriage.

She took her father's arm and they entered the Chapel together. The organ began to play, "*Here comes the bride*."

It was all over. Nothing could save her now. She was parted from her true love for ever.

She bid Roderick a silent, heartbroken farewell and began the journey down the aisle to where her bridegroom was waiting. Louisa moved as slowly as she could, because once she was married to Lord Westbridge her life would be over.

He watched her every step of the way. A smile of greed and self-satisfaction playing over his lips.

At last she reached him and reluctantly offered him her hand. His own hand was cold and clammy. She shuddered.

The Vicar cleared his throat and began to speak.

"Dearly beloved, we are gathered together to join this man and this woman – "

Louisa listened to the words in a trance. Beneath the heavy veil, tears glistened on her cheeks as Roderick and all the love and joy he had given her faded from her life.

"If any of you know of just cause or impediment," the Vicar intoned, "why this man and this woman may not be joined in holy matrimony, you are to declare it."

"Stop this wedding!"

Everyone turned at the imperious voice from the door. Louisa shouted with joy.

"Roderick!"

He stood there, proud and determined, his right hand raised. His face was bruised and frightfully pale, but his head was held high. As he strode down the aisle, Louisa noticed that three men accompanied him. One was Compton, Lord Hatton's private secretary. One was a policeman. Louisa recognised the third man as one of the guards from the asylum.

"This man belongs in a prison cell," Roderick declared. "He must answer to the law for his crimes."

"He is mad," Lord Westbridge howled.

The asylum guard stepped forward. "Lord Cranford is not mad," he stated firmly. "He has been your victim, as my own father has been. And he – " he pointed to the secretary, "has the evidence."

All eyes turned to Compton. The secretary, whom Louisa had thought so unpleasant, drew himself up. Suddenly he possessed a dignity she had not noticed at their earlier meeting.

He brandished a bundle of papers.

"It is all here," he announced. "All the details of his evil-doing. Cheating, fraud and outright theft. Enough to put him away for the rest of his life. I have allowed him to make me a part of his deeds, but now I hate what I have become."

Lord Westbridge let out a roar and tried to make a dash for the door. But quick as a flash the policeman snapped a pair of handcuffs on him.

"I arrest you on charges of fraud, theft – "

Lord Westbridge's face was ghastly as his wicked deeds caught up with him and in front of such a distinguished gathering.

Louisa stood transfixed, hardly able to believe that all this was happening.

The policeman finished reading out the charges. The wedding guests listened to him, astonished.

"This wedding is over," the policeman informed them. "The bridegroom has an urgent appointment, which will detain him for some years."

"I will make you sorry for this outrage!" Lord Westbridge snarled at the world in general.

"We will be leaving now, sir." The policeman addressed Compton. "Bring those papers to the Police Station," he ordered.

Compton gathered them up. He was smiling.

"I don't understand," Louisa gasped. "You are on *our* side? But I thought – "

"You thought I would betray you, when I saw you pass the letter to my daughter," Compton said.

"Jenny is your daughter?"

"I introduced her into Lord Westbridge's house to make it easier for me to smuggle messages in and out. She gave your letter to me."

"But what did it contain?" Louisa asked.

"Sending me to that asylum was the most foolish move Westbridge could have made," Roderick said. "George here – " he indicated the guard, "has suffered from his thievery too. Westbridge stole a large sum of money and managed to get George's father blamed for his misdeed."

"He is in prison for that theft now," George said. "I swore I would avenge him and bring that devil to justice."

"So George believed my story and helped me to escape," Roderick added.

"I told Lord Cranford what Westbridge had done to my family," George said. "Only Compton could find the proof, but I could not make contact with him myself. That letter told him what to look for."

"I knew that Westbridge had found out about the empty cottage," Compton said. "I sent Jenny with a message to George – "

"And George whisked me out of the cottage just in time," Roderick finished. "He has been hiding me while Compton put the last of the evidence together.

"There are papers that will free his father from Westbridge's clutches. The demon even keeps a book of whom he has cheated at cards, how and by how much."

Louisa gave a cry of joy. The miracle had happened and the darkness had passed.

Roderick took Louisa into his arms.

"It is all over, my darling," he said. "Thank God I did not arrive too late! That monster is defeated and now we can be together."

"Together," she murmured. "Together for all eternity!"

It was too much happiness. Louisa burst into tears and threw herself into his arms.

"Let us leave this place at once," Roderick said.

"But whatever are we going to do?" Lady Hatton moaned. She was too confused to understand what had just happened.

Now Roderick spoke with proud authority, like the Earl that he indeed was.

"We will go to your home, so that Louisa can change out of her clothes. Then we will all go to the Police Station and see this business through to the end."

He took Louisa's hand and led her out of the Chapel. She followed him gladly.

Her head was spinning with the speed of events, but when they reached the Police Station she was beginning to believe it was all true.

Lord Westbridge was like a cornered rat, bellowing his rage as the evidence piled up against him. The papers were damning. Every theft and fraud he had committed was written down in detail.

"I am reclaiming Cranford Manor at once," Roderick declared. "I want to prepare *my* home for *my* bride."

He held Louisa's hand tightly as he faced Lord and Lady Hatton.

"She is mine," he said proudly. "I shall never give her up."

Lord Hatton's eyes were wet with tears.

"If that is Louisa's wish – " he began.

"It is, Papa. Oh, it is!"

"Then take her with her father's blessing. And accept our thanks, sir, for what you have done to save us."

Louisa raised a glowing face to Roderick. The dreadful nightmare was over. Now their perfect happiness could begin.

*

It was Roderick's dream and Louisa's too, that they should be married at Christmas. It seemed impossible that everything could be accomplished in time, but now Roderick had powerful friends who would help him.

A Bishop came to marry them. He was an old friend of Roderick's grandfather and could also verify his identity.

The manager of the local bank, anxious to secure Lord Cranford as a customer, assured him of unlimited credit until his affairs were settled.

Many of the servants at the manor remembered old Lord Cranford with affection and they cheered the young Earl as he returned to claim his inheritance.

When he told them how he wanted the house to look for his bride, they scurried to please him. For them too, better times had arrived.

"I have plans for the estate," Roderick said. "I want to establish a school for all children – not just the tenants' offspring, but also the children of the servants. Why should the poor be denied the benefit of education? And I want only the best to teach them. A man with an Oxford degree would suit me."

His eyes, full of amusement, were on Simon.

"There is a nice little house that goes with the job. You can take possession immediately and I will pay your salary at once, so that you can support your wife while you finish University."

"But – I don't have a wife," Simon stammered, his eyes flying involuntarily to Arabelle.

Roderick grinned.

"That is for you to take care of, my dear fellow. I will leave the matter in your capable hands!"

He seized Louisa and they ran out of the room, leaving Simon and Arabelle in each other's arms. Soon they were similarly engaged.

*

But one issue clouded Louisa's joy. She felt that her parents were not at ease with her as they prepared for her wedding to Lord Cranford.

"They seem to be keeping their distance," she said unhappily to Roderick. "I thought they had accepted our marriage."

"I believe they are ashamed of the way they have treated you," he said. "They are afraid that they have caused you to hate them."

"They are my mother and father. How could I ever hate them?"

She heard a sob outside the door and ran out to find Lord and Lady Hatton standing there.

"Oh, my darling," her mother wept. "How could we have done it to you?"

"We were so very frightened," admitted Lord Hatton. "But that does not excuse us. How can we even beg for your forgiveness?"

"You do not need to beg for it," Louisa said. "You have it freely. All I ask is that you accept my husband and love me as you have always done."

She added joyfully,

"It is Christmas, the time for love and peace. Let us all be happy and forget everything that came between us."

She embraced both her parents. Now she could go to her wedding with a light heart. There was to be only peace and love.

*

At last, on Christmas Day, Louisa was ready to travel to the Chapel again to become the Countess of Cranford.

The dress she wore this time was very different to the over lavishness of her first wedding dress. It was made of very expensive lace, but cut on simple lines.

Jenny helped her to put it on. She had come to Louisa

and said that she would indeed like to become her lady's maid.

"But I was afraid that you didn't really mean it," she admitted. "You were just talking until you could give me the letter."

Jenny's eyes were bright and Louisa realised that she was not at all stupid. She had been pretending.

"My mother's maid has been looking after me," Louisa had said. "But I will really need someone else when I am married. I should like it to be you, Jenny."

Arabelle was to be her bridesmaid. Her own wedding would be the following month, when her parents had arrived from France. In the meantime she was joyful for her friend's great day, the day she and Simon had done so much to bring about.

It was time to leave for the ceremony and her mother and Arabelle drove on ahead to the Chapel, where Lady Hatton was escorted, by Lord Cranford himself, to the place of honour at the front.

Then Lord Hatton handed his daughter into the carriage and together they proceeded to her wedding.

Louisa gasped when she saw the chapel door, which had been decorated with Christmas roses. Arabelle was waiting for her. She adjusted the bride's veil, smoothed down her skirts and took her place behind her.

Everybody on the estate was present to cheer the bride's arrival. They were all so glad that their Master was now to be the Earl of Cranford and not the hated Lord Westbridge. And they were even gladder that Louisa, whom they knew and loved, would be their Mistress.

As she started the long walk up the aisle the organist began to play, very softly. The Bishop was waiting before the altar and there was Lord Cranford – no, her beloved Roderick – waiting for her.

As they knelt before the altar and the Bishop joined them together as man and wife, she felt that they were being blessed by God.

Now they repeated in public the vows they had made in private and all the world knew that they belonged to each other.

She had never known anything like the wonder and glory of this moment, when she finally became the wife of the man she adored.

'I love you, I love you,' she was saying to her husband, over and over again.

She knew that secretly he was saying the same to her.

At last the organ pealed out bright notes of triumph. The new husband and wife turned to leave the Chapel. As they emerged into the pale winter sun, the estate children threw flowers over them.

A large crowd had gathered. They cheered the bride and groom to the echo as they hurried the short distance to the house. They climbed the steps to the front door and turned to wave at the crowd. There was applause and another cheer which almost seemed to shake the building.

There were shouts of "good luck!" from some, while others called out "Happy Christmas!"

A band, which had come from the village, now started to play.

The bride and bridegroom escaped into the house, and all those who could not follow were served with cakes and mulled wine. As they made their way back to their homes they sang the songs of love and happiness which were always sung at Christmas.

As the Earl and his new Countess walked to the banqueting hall in which they were to receive their guests, Roderick said very quietly, so that only Louisa could hear,

"Now, my darling, you know that you are mine for eternity and we must never lose each other."

"I will never lose you," Louisa sighed. "At the moment we were married, I sensed that we were very close to God and that He blessed us both."

"I felt that too," he replied. "My precious, how could we ask more than that we should be blessed with love at Christmas, which is, as we both agree, the time of love."

"I love you," Louisa murmured very softly.

He lifted her hand to his lips as he said,

"I will tell you later, my darling, how much I love you and how blissfully happy I am that now you are mine for ever and ever."

Roderick had not allowed her to enter the house while it was being prepared for the wedding. He had said there was to be a surprise.

Now she could see his surprise and marvelled as she realised how much trouble he had taken for her.

Cranford Manor bore almost no resemblance to the place she had hated when it belonged to Lord Westbridge. Everywhere was decorated with flowers. There were flowers on every picture. Flowers entwined the banisters from the top to the bottom.

"I feel as though I am dreaming," she whispered into his ear. "How could you have made it look so wonderful in such a short time?"

"I did it all for you, my darling," Roderick answered.

He added,

"I must tell you that no one has ever looked more glorious, more beautiful or more adorable than you do at this moment."

He paused before he continued,

"All I want to do is hold you in my arms and kiss you.

But that will have to wait until we are alone."

She remembered how he had kissed her in the past. She recalled the feeling of excitement and passion which his kisses had brought her.

As if he had read her thoughts, Roderick said,

"I want to kiss you again, my darling, until we both realise that there is nothing more wonderful for us than each other. That is something which we will find for the rest of our lives."

"I love you, I adore you," Louisa managed to sigh.

Her feelings for Roderick were so intense and so sublime that it was difficult for her to breathe.

As they had knelt in the Chapel, she had been praying that her husband would always love her as much as he did today. In her heart she vowed always to be the perfect wife for him.

She realised that the trials they had endured to be together would make the bonds that united them stronger than ever.

They sat side by side at their wedding feast, smiling and behaving graciously to their guests. But secretly they longed to be alone.

Louisa gave thanks for her happiness and for the happiness of others that had also come to pass.

There, among the guests, was George, who had now left the asylum and come to work for Lord Cranford. And there was his father, newly released from prison.

And all over the country there were other victims of Lord Westbridge, whose Christmas would be happier for the knowledge that he had been brought to justice.

At last the feast was over. Night had fallen. The most blessed night of the year.

Alone in the great bedchamber, they stood together at

the window, looking out over the snow.

Roderick wrapped his arms around his bride.

"Where shall we go for our honeymoon?" he asked.

"What does it matter? I am already in Heaven."

"And I. But I want to take you to the ends of the earth and back. I want to show you all the wonders of the world.

"And then we shall look into our hearts, and know that we carried the wonders of the earth within us all the time. And no gift can ever be greater than the gifts we now give to each other."

"We will make our own Heaven on earth," Louisa murmured. "And there is nothing more that we could possibly ask."

Her words faded as Roderick's arms tightened around her. His lips touched hers and Heaven on earth was theirs.